AN ARAB MELANCHOLIA

SEMIOTEXT(E) NATIVE AGENTS SERIES

© 2012 by Semiotext(e)
© 2008. Originally published by Éditions du Seuil in Paris, France, under the
title *Une mélancolie arabe*.

Published by Semiotext(e)
2007 Wilshire Blvd., Suite 427, Los Angeles, CA 90057
www.semiotexte.com

Special thanks to Noura Wedell and Sarah Wang.

Cover Photography: Denis Dailleux, Agence Vu
Back Cover Photography: Abdellah Taïa by Ulf Andersen
Design: Hedi El Kholti

ISBN: 978-1-58435-111-5
Distributed by The MIT Press, Cambridge, Mass. and London, England
Printed in the United States of America

10 9 8 7 6 5 4 3 2

AN ARAB MELANCHOLIA

a novel

Abdellah Taïa

Translated from the French by Frank Stock

\<e\>

For Mustapha, my brother

I

I REMEMBER

It was my second chance at life. I had just found out what it meant to die. I had passed on. Then I came back.

I was running, running. Fast, fast. Fast, fast.

Where was I headed? Why? I don't know right now. I don't remember everything. To tell you the truth, I don't remember anything now. But it will come back to me. I know it will.

I see words, I hear voices. I see this image, this same red and yellow image again and again.

It's blurred. Eventually it will become clear. I'm waiting. I don't write anymore. I'm on my little bed. I'm trying to fill up the pages in my private journal. A future book. I'm concentrating. I'm forcing myself to go back to that moment, that racing off. That chase. I'm not breathing anymore. I close my eyes. I concentrate more. I curl up and try to distinguish those voices from another world that come to me with such racket, and then suddenly, stop. I go limp.

I'm afraid. I look up at the sky, then down at my slightly dirty feet.

It's starting to come back to me, back into my head, into my memory, into my body. Into my fingers. I can feel it, I can feel it. It's coming back, it's coming. I am happy. I am excited. My heart is thrilled. My skin loses its tension. I raise my head, I open one eye and look at what is coming down.

It's me. A young me. A teenager back in the '80s. A large backpack pressed against my stomach, I move through time, seconds, minutes, at full speed. In a race. I've only got one thing on my mind. One obsession. Souad Hosni, the mythical, beautiful, beyond beautiful Egyptian actress. Something real. My reality. I'm in a rush to enter my other life, my imaginary, true life, where I can commune with her, begin to find my unknown soul in hers.

I'm running faster and faster. I run for a long time. My mouth, wide open, gulps in air. I no longer feel my big feet. I no longer feel my nose, which is still small. I no longer feel any part of me. I am moving beyond myself. I am no longer solid. Soon I'll start to fly, soar over the boundaries between worlds. Disappear into the clouds, come back down and see, see myself.

From my first life, my first lifetime, my childhood spent being naked, alone naked, sometimes naked in a group, just one smell remains, a strong, human, disturbing, possessive smell. It's my mother M'Barka's smell. The smell that comes from her country-girl, slightly overweight body, the one which tells me that she hasn't bathed in a week. A smell that comes from the same place we do. Her, me. Tadla—that small town which the Oum Rabii River runs through. I am with her in her body. Like her, I come from that region, which I have never known. Never breathed in. But through M'Barka, that world of yesterday pulses through me today, throbs as I race towards my home and outwards to the faraway, the light, but soon happy dream of another life, the one that started before I began.

A meeting. A fusion.

I had just finished dying, dying in my bare feet.

I remember it now, all of it.

I can write about it.

It was summer, high summer. August, August the 7th. It happened during vacation, during the long summer vacation that each day turned me crazy and feverish.

My parents were sleeping. The entire Hay Salam neighborhood was taking a siesta. Only the men who sold loosies resisted the urge to sleep. There they stayed at the corner of the *derb*, loyal, waiting, hoping, their small transistor radios tuned to the Tangier station, Medi 1. I loved them. From a distance. I never spoke to them. I found them appealing. They were bad boys. Real tough guys. The damned. The scarred. Every night they drank cheap wine while they listened to their great diva, Oum Kalthoum. I am still in love with them. I can't get them out of my mind. Men around 20 or 30 years old, lean, tough, badly shaven, tender in spite of themselves. I have taken them with me. They are still strong within me.

I was walking to the dead ends of Lot 14, not sure what I was looking for. Maybe some kind of adventure. Some miracle. Looking for a friend of mine who had the same first name as me, Abdellah, the son of Ssi Aziz. He was two years older than me. A real adolescent who already sported a small, dark moustache. Unlike me, he always ended up ejaculating milk when he masturbated. On several occasions, he invited me to witness this private ceremony, an extraordinary show. At night, he and I, Abdellah times two, established this forbidden pleasure as our ultimate goal. His eyes closed, head thrown back, lips trembling one against the other, his cock large, thick, erect between the fingers of his left hand and the milk, a small amount of milk, shooting out in several spurts that ran and ran. My eyes were eager to take in the whole show, to retranscribe every movement, every sound of Abdellah's choreography, to note his pleasure, his orgasm and how the world stood still, how life stopped around us so that life itself could witness a miracle. Abdellah, my friend, my buddy, transforming himself for me into this body that only existed because of love and because it could be loved. A body that made love to itself.

Abdellah was shorter than me.

Sometimes, in order to enhance his pleasure, Abdellah would take my head in his right hand and without saying a word, gently move it closer to his own face in a miraculous moment, pressing his hot, dribbling, half-open, famished, delighted lips tightly against my left cheek. A brotherly kiss. A kiss that lasted a while. A kiss that never ended.

I'd let him do it. Delighted. I was part of his orgasm. I was learning. Soon I'd imitate him, thinking of him when I was alone.

That day, Abdellah was taking a siesta too.

I knocked on his bedroom window three times. He did not answer. I waited a few minutes before I knocked again, three times, same as always, as we agreed to do it. His father, usually so nice, the very image of a pious man, opened the front door and in a furious voice chased me from the front step. "Go play somewhere else, you dog, you piece of shit... Go on, get out of here... Abdellah is sleeping now... Leave us alone, you bastard... Move it, I said get going... You poor trash... Get outta here..." It was a degree of violence that left me speechless. That day, Ssi Aziz was not a good Muslim.

I wasn't like every one else. I didn't like siestas.

I was 12 years old and sometimes, I'd still wander the streets without shoes and socks. My childhood wasn't over yet. My childhood will never leave me. A naked childhood. With the horrible friends I adored and played with every day, disobeying the rules, acting crazy. Stealing things. Killing birds and cats. Smoking and drinking red wine. I was just like them. I was one of them. We did the *nouiba*: each guy pleasuring the next. We'd lower our pants and make love in a group. I could be myself with them. Myself and someone different. I loved them, yes I did. I stayed with them even when they insulted me, called me effeminate, told me I was a *zamel*, a passive faggot.

Abdellah, Ssi Aziz's son, wasn't part of our group. He was different, he belonged to me. Always separate from the others. Close to me. But not that day.

Chased away by his father, humiliated, unable to understand how this man, a man who was piety personified, could have said such terrible things to me, could have turned out to be like all the other grown-ups, just a two-faced adult. I wandered the streets. Miserable. Abandoned by my friend. Poor. Barefoot. Feverish. Maybe even ill. Alone out there under the sun, the sun which has never loved me.

I had gone past Lot 14. Without planning on it, I was up near Lot 11. Far from my house, right in the middle of unknown territory, almost among enemies. Lot 11, next to the basketball court and a few feet away from the Zaki Prison, which was still under construction.

Misfortune was headed my way.

The place was deserted. Modest one- or two-story houses still being worked on, unfinished homes like an empty movie set, long forgotten, no sign of life, no traffic. That was Lot No 11.

It was Wednesday.

Death had signaled me out.

Death walked up to me. Had a good look. A closer look.

I headed towards it. I didn't see death waiting.

Three boys came up to me. Unexpectedly they were standing in front of me. They were barefoot too. This is how they greeted me, "Hi, Leïla! How ya doing, Le-Ï-la?"

I knew what they wanted. I knew what I was in for.

But I didn't know what to do.

They were bigger than me. One of them was handsome, arrogant, with a hint of a beard. He did the talking, knew what he wanted, gave the orders. He said, "You've got a nice ass!" He moved in swiftly, close, put one hand on my shoulder and started feeling my ass with the other one. He was shaking slightly. He hesitated. I could see it on his pretty face, he was determined to have his way. I was his prey. He wasn't going to let me get away that easily.

They began to tease me. "Where's your slit? Don't you have a slit in your ass?"

That made his friends laugh. Not him. He seemed serious, aroused by my ass. His face turned red and he started in again. "Answer me, Leïla! Answer me, little girl! Don't you have an ass pussy? Is that your problem? Well, we're going to give you one… And fast… C'mon… Come with us… You'll see… What we're going to do won't hurt that much…"

The other two fell in behind us. The handsome one, the man, the boss, the one in charge, pretended to be nice as he showed me where to go. "You see the red house at the end of the street? That's where we're going to consummate our marriage… You're going to follow me and I give you my word, I'll be nice and gentle with you."

He thought I was afraid.

Everything he suggested sounded pretty good to me. A chance to fool around a little, get through the afternoon and survive its insanity by having a shot at sex, especially sex with him. That wasn't the kind of offer I could turn down. I could already imagine the kind of things we'd do, the stuff we'd come up with, how we'd get naked. All that exploring. Touching. Small me. Big him. His scratchy beard. My ass turning him on. How we'd pleasure one another. Play around. Forget about playing around. We weren't children anymore. We'd have sex, real sex. Serious sex. He'd always be in charge. I'd let him think I was passive.

I was dreaming. Dreaming with my eyes wide open, with my eyes blind, rendered sightless by that merciless sun. I was happy. Picturing how things would be, feeling happy.

We had come to the two-story, red house. The front door wasn't completely closed. The good-looking one pushed it open gently, had us step inside one by one and showed us the stairs.

His parents must have been taking a siesta too. When I climbed the stairs, I heard the sound of a woman snoring.

"It's on the second floor. Go up and wait for me... I'll join you in a minute... And you, Leïla, be nice, otherwise my two friends are going to hurt you... bad... You got that? Let me say it again. Things will turn ugly, real ugly, if you don't let us do exactly what we want. You understand what I'm saying? Yes or no?"

I could have cried out. Saved myself. The woman who was snoring would have certainly come to my rescue. Set me free and given me back my true identity. Perhaps she would have given me something to eat and punished her bearded son in front of me.

I did nothing.

I climbed the stairs like the man in charge ordered me to. Submissive. Quite curious. What would happen now?

On the second floor, there was an empty apartment, completely empty except for one room with a big bed placed on the floor, a bed so new it was still in its plastic cover. The good-looking guy's two friends shoved me inside and closed the door behind me.

I was alone.

The room was dark. I could hardly see a thing. I didn't know where to stand.

I settled next to the door, waiting, standing, feeling strangely calm, compliant. A little like the sheep on Aïd el-Kébir an hour before they slit their throats.

Time stopped flying. No noises from the outside world. A world crushed beneath oppressive heat pressed against the cool room where I stood. After a few seconds, my eyes adjusted to the darkness in the room. I liked being protected from the sun, tucked away in the unknown with this place yet to be discovered and this story yet to be written. I had a good feeling and I did not fight it. Fear, the feeling I knew inside and out, left me in peace that day, at least for the moment.

The room was small and smelled like wet paint. You might even say that the plastic-covered bed, big, blue and directly in the middle of the room, looked like an indoor swimming pool. I could picture the water, hear the tiny waves. They were calling out to me. I quickly undressed, stripped down to nothing but my red underpants and jumped into bed, diving right in. But I didn't know how to swim. I just closed my eyes and relaxed.

I was asleep. I was floating. The world had turned blue and I was a little kid, then a big kid, and soon I was all grown up, seeing myself in a whole different light. I had created a whole new me, a whole new life.

I wasn't asleep. I was waiting. Lying on my stomach, I tried to picture the boy with the beard, the boy in charge of the group who had—yes, I had to face the facts—locked me up. He came to mind quickly and I could see him standing in front of me, shoes off, barefoot just like me, but much more masculine, more of a man than I was. He was telling me, "Stay in bed, I'm on my way… I'll be there… Rest… I'm bringing you some watermelon…" I wanted to ask him his name but he was already gone, out of the frame, out of the part of my dream that had seemed so real. All that was left was his smell, the smell of a boy who only took a bath once a week, and it lingered in my mind even though I never noticed it when I was with him.

I breathed in deeply. I knew his first name.

Chouaïb.

The same name as my cousin, whom I had been in love with for some time. Our families were never on good terms. Sometimes he'd defy their rules and show up at my house on his moped. I was in love with him, in love with his moustache, in love with his leather jacket, in love with his moped, a Peugeot 103 that he'd always ask me to ride on. Invite me to sit in front of him and head out someplace far from Hay Salam. I was in love with him then and I often helped him find dealers so that he could buy hash, kif, or else *maajoun*. I'd sit next to him in the courtyard of our house, sappy, thinking the world of him and then he'd carefully roll a joint, and I'd watch him slowly smoke the whole thing. He enjoyed himself and I would witness his transformation. Under the influence of the sweet drug, he'd start to smile, smile at himself, smile at the invisible world, the world of the *jinns*, a world I knew quite well, thanks to my mother and the things she loved. He'd smile at me, and I'd sit next to him already happy as I waited for the kiss I knew he'd give me, a kiss from him and his moustache.

I fell asleep. It was a kick, a kick in the side from bearded Chouaïb that woke me up, woke me right up. He had come looking for me without the others. On the bed, up close, I could really smell him, pick out the smell of his sweaty body, a body going through many changes day after day. The body of an adolescent who was tired of waiting and who wanted to become a man, fast—a big, strong, imposing man. That's what he'd be immediately: someone leaving his sweet and terrible childhood, someone shaking off adolescence and all its hell. Chouaïb was in full metamorphosis. I could see it, feel it, understand it better than he did.

He was next to me. His eyes were red, full of anger. His was staring at me. All he saw was me and he didn't like what he saw.

"It's my turn now!"

That wasn't what I had expected. I thought that something in me could make him tender, sensitive, bring him back to a sweeter version of himself. Nothing like that happened. Nobody came to my rescue. Chouaïb? He didn't seem like the same person anymore. It was his turn now. That was what he said, twice, forcing himself to be violent. With a mean look still in his eyes, he added, "You ready for it?"

I couldn't think of anything to say. I looked him straight in the eye. I wanted him to understand that I wasn't afraid. I wanted him to know that in another situation, another place, I would have been proud and happy to let him take me, but here under his rule, all I could do was obey him regardless of how I felt, obey his orders without a single stirring of pleasure.

He couldn't read the message in my eyes. He had a nervous, exaggerated laugh. He blurted out, "I see you're only wearing underpants… And red ones at that… Well, it looks like you're ready to get started… Aren't you… I'm coming… You ready for it?"

And he started.

In a violent downward swoop, he yanked my underwear off. With a prompt, no-nonsense shove, he flipped me over onto my stomach so that he could have full access to my ass. He bent over it so that he could smell it, knead it, bite it. He sat up, taking control of my ass, touching it, pinching it. He kept telling me, slowly saying, "I love your ass, I love your ass, Leïla!" My Leïla ass, whose sexual power I was just discovering, was out of my control. From then on, its fate was in Chouaïb's hands. I thought about telling him my real name, telling him I was a boy, a man just like him... Telling him that he turned me on, explaining that there was no need for violence between us. I'd let him do whatever he wanted, just as long as he stopped turning me into a woman... I wasn't Leïla. I wasn't his sister. I wasn't his mother. I was Abdellah, Abdellah from Lot 15 and, in a few days, I'd be 13.

I wanted to tell him a lot of things. My secret adventures. Words hot as summer. How I saw the situation, how the man in charge made me feel, the torrents he was beginning to release inside me. Along with fire. Blood. Ice. Wind. And most of all, I wanted him to know that despite everything they said about me in Hay Salam, how I was a "girlie boy," a "baby doll," despite all these treacherous names, I was still a virgin. A complete virgin. An ass virgin. Sure, I had already had sex, sex with boys my own age and sex with boys who had already reached manhood, but none of them had ever penetrated me. No one had ever been deep inside me.

I wanted to tell him repeatedly that a boy is a boy and a girl is a girl. Just because I loved men and always would, didn't mean that I was going to let him think of me as the opposite sex, let him destroy my identity, my history like that. Let him press up against me, in an utterly naked moment, and not have to find out the first thing about me, without understanding a single thing about me. Sex was one thing. Maybe we would have gotten it on somewhere else. But letting him call me Leïla, forget that, no way. I wasn't about to be turned into a girl just so I could make the guy happy. Even though I was already starting to like him, forget it, there was just no way. None. That would have been a complete betrayal of everything I stood for, a betrayal of all the things I've constructed for myself since I was born, an act of treason against my legend, an act of supreme disloyalty to my romantic dream, to all my possessions, treason against my sex itself. A betrayal of the force that moves me forward, guides me, and knows me better than I know myself, the force which I am not about to abandon.

Despite all that, I had always liked Leïla as a first name. Thanks to an 8th century poet known as El Majnoun, The Crazy One, I knew the importance Arabs attached to the name in both literature and imagination. El Majnoun wandered around possessed by the *jinns* of poetry, and he was so madly in love with the beautiful Leïla that history only speaks of his thwarted love, his magnificent obsession, recorded forever in those poems he wrote for her, sublime love poems that reveal neither his true identity nor any other facts about his life. But all Arabs, even the ones who have never read his poems, are very familiar with Majnoun-Leïla, know who he was and respond to his texts with sympathy and admiration.

Leïla's father was rich. He kept his daughter prisoner. He did not want her marrying Majnoun. Condemned to endless wandering, Majnoun allowed the desert he roamed to bring his life to an end. People sometimes say that Majnoun never existed, but his immortal poetry proves them wrong. He lives on, still very much alive in our minds.

Chouaïb was naked now, completely naked. His cock was erect, and all by itself it started poking around for an entranceway between my ass cheeks. That's when I finally realized what was going to happen to me, physically, inside me. There would be an explosion. My first one.

I closed my ass.

I closed my eyes.

Forced them shut.

I could feel Chouaïb on top of me. He was heavy. He wasn't himself anymore. I could smell him everywhere. The sweat from his body mixed with my own. We were already joined, joined together whether he wanted to be or not.

He wanted more than that. He wanted to really fuck me, push it right in.

He leaned over me two or three times, pretended he was a nice guy and then told me, "O-pen up... open up, Leïla... Give me your ass, give it to me, because I'm going to take it anyway... Come on, Leïla, open that thing up... my dick is going to slide in there, you'll see... Come on, open it up, open..."

His cock grew harder and harder. It stuck straight out. He was ready, ready to attack me, but I wouldn't surrender. He grabbed me by the head, pulled my hair back, and in a tough-guy, I'm-the-man-in-charge voice told me, "Open your ass, I said, open it... Open your ass or I'm going to have to rape you. I swear, little Leïla, I will rape you."

I opened my eyes. I turned and shouted in his face, "My name's not Leïla... I'm not Leïla... I'm Abdellah... Abdellah Taïa..."

He was shocked. He'd finally figured it out. What he saw in my eyes had nothing to do with fear or submission.

It didn't make him change his plans.

He slapped me. Slapped me hard.

My head was pounding, but I didn't cry.

Instead, I punched him in the stomach without giving it a second thought.

We started fighting, more violently than before. And this time, I wasn't happy to just hold my own. No, I turned into a ferocious little wildcat.

That's what he liked, brawling. Brawling where each boy lost a little. Brawling where each boy went on the attack. He was really getting turned on, more and more aroused.

And I was too. Getting angry, getting hard.

We slugged it out, real punches, pretend punches. He called me all kinds of names: *zamel*, candy-ass, bitch, his little Leïla. I started biting him, biting him on the arms, the thighs. We were pushing and shoving. We rolled on top of one another, one of us crushing the other against the bed, the floor. This wasn't a game anymore. It was all about honor. Our honor as men. The honor we'd have to live with tomorrow.

I hated Chouaïb. Nothing about him appealed to me now. But I wanted to stay like this forever: naked, stretched out under another man, skin against skin, alive in the chaos of an intimate, sexual war.

The entire time I was punching him, trying to be as clever and cruel as he was, I knew deep down that I had a soft spot for him, that I could see myself falling in love with him once it was all over. Asking him to marry me. Being his.

Chouaïb could see that things weren't going as planned. He wasn't in charge anymore. I had fought back. Without his thugs-in-training, I thought he might become affectionate any minute. Act a little sweet. Act a little feminine. See the whole afternoon in a different light. See sex in a different light. He didn't want anything to do with any of that. He went on being the boss. He said, "You belong to me… You're mine… And I'm going to rape you… Got that?"

I understood perfectly well, but there was no way I was going to surrender, no way I'd let myself be his little slave again, his little Leïla.

The fight lasted about fifteen minutes.

We were both out of breath.

He got up and went over to the door. Like a real coward, he said, "I'm not going to rape you all by myself… We're all going to rape you… We're all going to make a real girl out of you…"

He opened the door.

I was standing in fear up to my waist. A fear that kept rising. A fear that was starting to drown me. A fear that made me blind.

The others walked in. There were four of them now, not just two, like when the whole incident started. It was dark in the room so I couldn't see what the new boys looked like. They took their clothes off immediately. The sex party was about to begin. Chouaïb was proud of himself. "Let's go boys, he's all ours."

I felt more and more afraid. In their control. Helpless. Alone. Unable to defend myself. No way to fight back.

So I gave in.

There stood Chouaïb, right in the middle of his boys. Chouaïb the big shot once again, the man in charge. Chouaïb the man, the man hiding behind a mask. Big tough Chouaïb, the man who showed no mercy.

He was the winner.

They moved in closer and began masturbating.

I stretched out on my back in the middle of the blue bed.

I closed my eyes. I tried to picture the pool again, the water, the chlorine, the diving board, the peacefulness, the luxury. An impossible dream for me at the time.

I was swimming, swimming in 15 feet of fear. I was shaking, trembling inside. I could no longer see them, but I could sense it when the boys gone bad approached my body, circling around to sniff at it, lick it. Any minute now, they'd start their sexual assault. One by one, they were ready to make me bleed. Put their mark on me. Take away any dignity I had left. Break me.

They were breathing hard. They smelled. It was hot up there. The heat and sweat rippling from their bodies turned the room into a steam bath, an oven. They spat into their hands. Laughing. They had stopped talking. They were all over me. All five of them. I knew which one was Chouaïb. I had already memorized the way his skin felt, how soft it was, how dry.

They were almost inside me. Showed no consideration.

That's when God stepped in. That's the moment when God saved me.

The *muezzin* from the neighborhood mosque started the Al-Asr call to prayer. We had no trouble hearing him. He sounded so close, his voice filled the room. What a beautiful voice he had, mellow. As he called us all to prayer, he sang out to God with fervor and emotion.

The *muezzin* wasn't taking a siesta.

Chouaïb shouted to his friends, "Stop! Stop! Let's wait until the *muezzin* finishes... It wouldn't be right to do this while he's still calling the faithful... Can't we just wait..."

He was obviously a good Muslim. He feared God. He respected the Prophet Mohammed. He could never worship sex and God at the same time. Never. They each had their place.

Despite the dim light in the room, God could see us. Five naked boys, penises hard and soft in their hands. And a sixth boy, nude and ambiguous, a boy about to be sacrificed.

I was a good Muslim too. I really thought of myself as a good Muslim back then. I feared God, feared hell and suffering after death. I feared the Dark Angels. I loved the Prophet, loved the story of his life and all the sayings attributed to him. Along with my mother, I venerated the saints and their holy tombs.

I was a street kid, superstitious, kind of different, a little crazy.

Like Chouaïb, I didn't mix God and sex, mix what was pure with what was impure.

I loved them both. Separately.

I loved Chouaïb.

I admired him for what he had just done.

The *muezzin* took his time reminding us that God existed, that God was powerful. His chanting was overwhelming. Deeply moving. It struck me again how simple it was. How beautiful. How accessible.

Once the call to prayer ended, the boys were as horny as ever and went back to work. They started masturbating. Chouaïb wanted to get hard again. He climbed on top of me, mounted my ass. I felt his hard body again, felt his cock start to grow little by little. I didn't resist, not any more. I was his for the taking. He was going to rape me.

This time I was ready for him, ready to take him.

Then we heard a voice. A woman was calling a boy.

"Ali… Ali… Aaali… Aliiiii…"

Chouaïb stopped rubbing against me immediately.

That's how I learned his name.

He didn't answer. The woman started calling for him again, calling out his name. "Ali… Ali… AAAli… Ali, my son, are you upstairs?"

Ali let his full weight collapse against me. He went limp, maybe he was angry.

The woman, who must have been his mother, started up

the stairs that led to the second floor. She kept calling her son, the boy slumped over me. "Ali, Ali, my son, come here, come downstairs, I need you to run an errand... You have to go to the store... We're out of donuts and it's almost snack time."

Her voice sounded closer and closer.

Ali shot up.

Ali jumped off my body.

Ali left me there.

Ali left without even looking at me.

I had ceased to exist for Ali.

He ran to the door as fast as he could, opened it halfway and yelled back, "Coming, mom... Be right there... You don't have to come up..."

And there I sat, all alone, lying in the triumphant sunlight that blinded me. The basketball court was still empty. I wandered around as the streets started to fill up again. Siesta time was over. I had no idea where to go, where to stop. My ears were ringing with the last thing Ali had said to me before he set me free.

"Next time, Leïla, I won't let you down. I won't."

I wished I were born a woman. A real woman.

I wished I were crazy. Really crazy.

Because that's how I was going to turn out some day. As crazy as the pirates from Salé who went around terrorizing people back in the 17th and 18th centuries. Become a crazy privateer, a captain of his own sweet dream who tried to give his dream a keel, who invited others to sail along, who shouted out his dreams, writing down every detail in his log.

I was a wreck. I was confused. All sorts of thoughts raced through my mind. I couldn't control myself. I was walking along, nice and calm, and I'd get angry, then I'd be quite civil, and then I'd be right in your face with my defiance. I knew too well the kind of life people would expect me to live, off in the margins somewhere. I already knew the level of private and public shame that would follow me everywhere. And I said, no way. There's no way I'm going to put up with either scenario. But I couldn't verbalize it, couldn't force people to accept it.

From now on, people would only see me one way. I'd come with a warning label. A tag: effeminate guy. Sissy. They wouldn't take me seriously. People would take advantage of me every day, abuse me more and more. In their own small way, people would kill me. Slay me alive.

I was in love, or to put it in other words, I was going to have a fight on my hands. Ali, who finally did show me a little affection, who finally wound up pitying me in the end, well, he didn't have a clue. I'd have to tell him, spell it out for him. I was as good as dead, so why not risk everything, risk every last bit of it, starting right now? All at once, I wasn't afraid to tell everybody my deep, dark secret, I couldn't care less about the scandal it would cause in Hay Salam. I could do what I wanted.

This voice, my voice, for the first time in Arabic, said, "I love you!"

Now Ali needed to hear these words.

I remembered how to get to Ali's house. I was already

connected to his place, had made up my mind about it, was angry and happy about it, and I don't know why, I just stood there. There in the distance, I could see Ali's red house, directly in front of me. I knew that was the place where I'd face who I was, turn my destiny around out loud. That house would be the stage for my big, dramatic scene and the denouement to follow. I couldn't help staring at it, noticing how much it looked like the house my family lived in. I gazed at it, lovingly. I also noticed what was going on around me. People were looking at me. That's what a Moroccan street was like. A nice little place dominated by morality and fear, a place I both loved and hated, the place where I was going to out myself completely in front of everybody, really shake them up, shock them, make a big scene. That's where I'd calm myself down again, finally feel relieved, start to live according to my newfound morality, start to write about my newfound life.

I was standing right next to an electric pole, a metal conductor filled with high-voltage wires. Big. Very tall. And so familiar. Like a childhood toy.

I was about to take off, fly away, write about something different, live out my love in broad daylight, proclaim my love, become the person people weren't even supposed to mention, the person who wasn't even supposed to exist. As I was leaving, I don't really know why, I touched one of the power lines with my left hand.

Electrocution.

Everything black.

Nobody around me.

Death.

Later on, other people would be the ones who would explain what had happened, who would again fill me in on this part of my life, tell me all about it.

Later on. Everything that these words *later on* used to mean would never be the same.

My life took a whole new direction. Something new, something interior and secret.

I was forced to take that route. I had no choice.

For the time being, I was dead.

Off in another world.

I don't remember anything about that world.

I opened my eyes.

The whole neighborhood had come to our house, everybody, all the neighbors from Lots 13, 14, 15.

They were crying. They were shouting.

There was a man in a white summer *jellaba* kneeling next to me. His head rested on my stomach. He was crying too. That was the first time I saw him cry. His voice sounded hoarse, but sweet at the same time. He was so tender. So overwhelmed. He forgot what men were not supposed to do. He knelt, crying, his tears soaking my T-shirt.

This man, this man who never talked much, this man who loved women and the Prophet, this man was my father. My kind father. My dear, sweet father, Mohammed.

They brought me back to the world.

My heart started beating again.

I opened my eyes fully. I saw my father, my own father.

I cried out, "I love you!"

Mohammed cried out too, "Get me some hot water, fast, come on, fast... No, not cold water, not cold..."

He knew how to keep me alive. Safe at home.

He was the one who washed my face, my hands, my feet. The water was hot, boiling. It felt so good.

I was recovering. Little by little.

I started breathing again.

But I hadn't forgotten about my other life.

From now on, I'd tell my story alone, write about it in silence, away from other people, away from the evil eye. I'd be protected by my loving father and my mother who was something of a witch. I was in something else. I was becoming more and more odd. Even bizarre.

People stopped thinking of me as effeminate. Now I was the boy who had been granted a miracle.

For me, that marked a starting line. I'd break with the pack and really start to run. Run toward my dreams? Run to save my hide? My soul?

I was glad to run, not giving it a second thought. Oh, I'd run. And keep running.

I'd run without saying a word. Run without a finish line.

I'd run back to Ali who never talked to me again.

I'd run towards the unknown me, the one that was found, the lost self.

I'd run to discover the world of movies and wide-eyed worship in the temple of its images.

I'd run to escape the *jinns*, all the while hoping I'd see them one more time.

I'd run towards the small, insignificant, superficial things that brought me happiness day by day.

I had seen it. The dream was stronger than life.

I kept running. Sometimes my heart would stop beating. That's when I'd go to my mother and ask her to show me again how to pray like she did. Pray with reinvented rituals, reinvented dogmas. Pray in my own way.

I'd enter the race again. Always fast. Always at breakneck speed. Like that day, that one Saturday in winter after six, after class.

That's the day I was running towards an image, towards a woman. An Egyptian actress. A big star. A diva named Souad Hosni. She was on television, in a series I loved. In *Houa wa Hiya*: He and She. I was running towards her to embrace her. To spend an hour with her, become her teary-eyed lover, her dancing partner, the actor of my own life. To go to Cairo. Always Cairo. To live in a mix of fantasy and reality. Arab. Non-Arab. To learn how to live life to the fullest from her, feel every emotion, feel totally alive, alive despite the silence.

On Saturdays, she was the source of my happiness, my adolescent joy. Nothing else. A small gift of life given to me. So simple. A popular series. A legendary actress and me, the boy who ran and ran and was always running.

Alone. Distrustful. Nobody to confide in. Crazy. And with every step I took, more and more crazy. Out of breath with every step, happy, sad. My mind made up. Movies would be my life. Movies were what I was about, whether I liked it or not. And their truth was the only one that mattered. The one truth that would keep telling my story. Paying attention to my life and writing the whole script down.

II

I'M GOING THERE

I was on my way back from Marrakech where I had spent a week finishing a course on film production.

Paris, my adopted home for seven years, the place where I tried to discover who I was, tried to endlessly reinvent myself, was as it is each time I return, a difficult city to win back. It didn't stop raining and the walls of buildings turned even darker. Paris without sunshine, without a single *bonjour*. Paris stood empty despite the millions that lived there.

I wanted to go to sleep immediately. Forget all the drabness. Head someplace so I'd find the strength, the energy I needed to feel reconnected with the artificial, but nonetheless real, lights of the temperamental megalopolis. To fall asleep, to quickly imagine that I was back there with him, to prove to myself that I could remember him, every inch of him, even before I saw him again in the flesh, in just a few hours. Maybe a few days?

His name was Javier.

He was French with a Spanish background.

He was short, shorter than me. His head was shaved. He always dressed in a sexy ghetto style, as he would later point out.

The film was shot in the El-Badi Palace, not far from Jemaa el Fna Square in Marrakech, and he was the still photographer.

He didn't speak.

He watched me.

Sometimes, for three or five seconds, he looked me straight in the eye.

He smoked all the time.

He never budged from his corner of the set and I never knew when he was actually taking pictures.

He was like a solitary and mysterious visitor.

Every day, he'd watch me more and more insistently, but always with some detachment. I couldn't work anymore, couldn't concentrate as I should have been on what was being created around me, images of a young terrorist who is both Moroccan and Muslim.

He was the one who set up our little connection, but it was up to me to take the first step. I figured that out quickly. He was reeling me in, playing me from a distance, not making a move, drawing me closer with his bad-boy attitude and the cigarettes he smoked with grace and intensity.

He wasn't my type. Not at all. But he kept looking at me.

He had big, dark, deep eyes. When he aimed them at me, I didn't know what to do. I'd turn shy, become a polite little boy. It was like I was hypnotized, hypnotized in spite of myself by who-knows-what within him, a type of charm that was beyond my understanding, something that seemed to reside in his piercing and slightly ironic stare, something that moved me to rapture.

Of course I was flattered. But the things that really bothered me—the way my feelings were all mixed up, the fear I felt in the pit of my stomach—were things that went well beyond my narcissism.

Day after day, he was right in front of me. He never said hello. He never showed up to eat with me in the cafeteria. He was out there, right out there, constantly in my field of vision, mute, opaque. A cock tease maybe?

The other members of the crew had very quickly ceased to exist. All I could see was him. A statue with a sophisticated digital camera in his hands. An infrequent smile, stiff, radiant. The left hand that slowly passed, from time to time, across his shaved head. Young-looking, kind of like a puny adolescent, kind of like me. A small man who, instead of walking, skipped, danced. A stranger from whom I wanted nothing, but who with his very first glance, pushed me even further inside the territory where feelings become confused.

He wasn't my type, not really. But I was conquered heart and soul, my body and my days no longer my own.

I was aroused, somewhat happy, already suffering.

How was I going to approach him? Where? What would I say to him? How should I act in front of him? What did I have to say to get him interested? And what if he clammed up, how was I going to react? What should I tell him about myself, about me right now, about my past? Did he want to sleep with me, was that it, did he only want to sleep with me?

Was I in love with him?

Was he in love with me?

I dared to ask myself these last two questions two days before we finished filming. I didn't know how to answer. The only thing I was aware of was my growing distress, how sadness and happiness were fighting inside me.

I was only too familiar with my reactions inside the arena of love. I rushed right in. I don't like waiting. I believe in love at first sight. I need to know everything, everything right away. I'm not afraid of heartache. I don't like playing the game of seduction for long. I always want to know exactly how somebody feels about me. I'm too curious not to ask. I never know how to pretend... I take things very seriously, unfortunately.

I want to be in love.

I wanted to be in love and I wanted to be loved back and that was the exact moment when Javier appeared in my life, showed up in my homeland, right there on the red earth that had been red forever.

It wasn't his fault.

I forgive him.

I couldn't stay like that, with Paris completely indifferent and me starting to feel an extraordinary, totally shattering emotion. I was no longer in control, not on the inside. I already felt the impatience that love brings on, showed all the carelessness caused by love. His, his, I was completely his. My brain would come up with a thousand ways to get closer to him. To be in his presence. To stand in front of him and test how I really felt about him. To see how deep my attraction to him ran, to find out what it was about him that attracted me in the first place, moved me, inspired my imagination to concoct a thousand tales, and he was the hero in every one of them. To move closer to his skin, his scent, his shaved head, his cigarettes, his Andalusian eyes, his small body, his shy and greedy smile, his first name, Javier, to say it, say his name, say it in front of him, say in secret, then call him by his name, fill his name with meaning and importance, fill it with the both of us. To dream about him, dream about him in the real world, in the world of my own reality. And then to discover him. Find out what his apartment looked like, take it all in without passing judgment. To picture myself against the Parisian backdrop of his life, the life he led before he met me. To listen to his sounds. To discretely uncover all his little secrets.

I couldn't sleep. I was in a state of arousal, excited by the still-fresh memory of the last night we spent together before heading back to Paris, the overwhelming intensity of desire and raw emotion, our silence, our distance, then our coming together, body against body. Two fragrances. Scents that tried to blend together, fought, competed with one another so that they could be tamed… That night, for the first time, I was his and he was mine, when Marrakech, the red city, was there with us in all its heat, and soon would pass judgment upon our story, a temporary witness to our relationship, to a link I couldn't help but kindle, ignite by force and then step back, more surprised than anyone else, by the intensity of the blaze.

Inside my dark apartment, eyes wide open, on the verge of a panic attack, I kept telling myself that I had to take action, confront the issue head-on, find out what I meant to him, what I meant to both of us. Was there even an "us?" Get some kind of answer. A promise. A hint. A further connection. A sweet, straightforward smile.

I wasn't dreaming. I was laboring under love's dictatorship. I was speeding things up. I didn't want to wait. I had to force him to tell me how he felt. There was no other solution.

I especially had to tell him what had happened on the plane. Try to find the right words, the right emotion. Tell him how afraid I was, how close to death I came. My last breath.

That takeoff. And then how love, the love I felt for him, revealed itself without even asking. I had to tell him everything. Force him to listen.

Move him to tenderness.

I waited five days. Five days with a fever.

In two weeks, I was leaving again. This time for Cairo to work on a film.

Cairo, the cinema. And a reunion with the Arab World, this time in a way I'd never experienced before.

I was the one who called.

He invited me over to his place.

Ever since I met him, saw him, touched him, my life, my days, my nights could all be summed up in a single word: Javier. I dreamed about him all the time. I kept asking him, though he knew nothing about it, to play an important part in my life, to play his part in a love story, to follow my lead, to keep reassuring me. Not to go running off later like so many before him. Not to think of me as a hook up, only a sex partner. I had read too many books, seen too many films. My life and my emotions were more than I could handle.

I needed him back with me, needed him fast. I needed to convince myself that all the things that happened really did happen, that the alchemy was real, that those eyes really lit up. That the very unsettling experience I had on the plane had really happened and ushered me once again into this thing we call love. I needed to believe that this silent boy could somehow be the answer to my dreams and my prayers.

It was still raining in Paris. Javier lived next to the Montmartre Cemetery, a few feet away from Clichy Square.

A dreary rain was falling.

I needed to talk to him, rub up against him again, press my body against his and stand back a little so that the words could come spilling out, word after word—clear, trembling, honest.

A sad rain was falling.

It hadn't stopped raining since I had gotten back. Eventually, I liked the awful weather. It had become, as if by magic, romantic. Anyway, nice weather was out of the question. Forget it. The skies over Paris worked with me. We were accomplices, friends.

I went to his place.

It was night. He was tired. He smoked incessantly, always with the same great elegance.

I cried. He didn't see me.

How can I describe his apartment?

Three small rooms in a state of unbelievable disorder, and the smell that gave me a headache right way, the scent of his latest fragrance, "le Mâle" by Jean-Paul Gaultier. Techno music blared in the background as if to stop me from thinking. There he was in his sexy clothes, his shaved head shining, but not really there, like some kind of guest, some kind of distant relative passing through Paris. My presence didn't seem to matter. He offered me a drink, sparkling water, then hid behind his computer screen with two urgent e-mails that he had to send off.

Sitting in what served as the living room, I watched him. I recognized him, knew that it was really him, Javier, as small as in Marrakech and just as silent. Always a question mark. It was strange seeing him in Paris, but I didn't know why. On the other hand, seeing him immediately detached and distant helped me understand that the time we had spent together, our glances and our bodies there so attracted, and here so distanced, meant nothing to him.

That wasn't how I felt.

I knew what I was in for: heartache, aching for an indefinable someone who, even though he didn't say it, even now, wanted nothing more to do with me.

Marrakech was like a vacation for him.

Well, Marrakech wasn't my hometown but it was my country.

He sat there drumming on the keyboard.

I waited. Fifteen minutes. Half an hour. An eternity.

Humiliated.

I was nothing but a hook up. The kind of man who gets too clingy, who doesn't figure things out fast enough, who's always looking for something more. A real nuisance. The kind of guy who becomes sentimental and thinks everything that happens means something. How was he going to dump me?

That's what he was trying to figure out.

He didn't look at me. His tasteless techno music, that mindless repetition of electronic sounds, filled the entire apartment and did what Javier himself couldn't do. It built a wall of separation between us, a border that would keep us apart from now on.

I knew that. I got it.

I started to cry. Cry for myself. Because I had been so stupid, so naive. I cried because he was the man I once thought about constantly, cried because, in his mind the bond between us was only imaginary, something that didn't exist, even though unfortunately, I found our connection real and entirely thrilling.

I cried, but the tears did not run down my cheeks.

He stood up suddenly, looked at me, smiled and as he passed in front of me, rested his hand on my hair for two seconds.

He could do something like that.

He was using the bathroom. I could hear him pissing. It took a long time. Another eternity.

The only thing I could do was leave, get out of there.

He came out of the bathroom and once again put his hand on my head for a brief moment as he walked past.

Then, enjoying every minute of it and acting like he cared, he said, "One more e-mail, then we'll fuck."

I was blown away!

That was all I meant to him.

That's what the whole thing was about: hooking up and fucking. All the ups and downs my heart rode out and my imagination went through, and this was where it got me.

Of course I wanted more. I expected more, more from him and more from life.

I got up.

I walked slowly towards him and kissed him on the fore-head. I kissed Javier, the man I carried in my mind and in my heart. The fictitious Javier, but who was real to me. I kissed Javier so that I could touch him one last time, walk away with one shared memory, a memory of him, of us.

And I walked out, left without saying goodbye. Left without going back. Left without hearing from him again.

Left without talking about what had happened on the plane.

I wanted to get sick.

I walked in the rain.

It was dark.

It was December, close to Christmas. Paris would be transformed from one day to the next by the magical lights that in spite of everything, would cheerfully mark the end of the year. The city was cloaked in rain. Like me. But each garbed in our own solitude.

I was living in Belleville. To get home, I could catch the subway at Clichy Square, take Line 2 in the direction of Nation. That's not what I did. I didn't want anybody looking at me, figuring out how unhappy I was. Seeing me right after someone had just dumped me, once again. Seeing how wrong I was about things. I didn't want to make a spectacle of myself. I just wanted to walk around, breathe in the night alone, walk across the city, the place I came to when I left Morocco to pursue my dreams of breaking into the movies, the home where I found myself happy and sad again and again, found myself still standing with both feet on the ground.

It was a direct route. No sidetracks. Blanche. Pigalle. Anvers. Barbès-Rochechouart. La Chapelle. Stalingrad. Jaurès. Colonel-Fabien. Belleville. Nine metro stations on foot. A walk across Paris. My very own Stations of the Cross, which I followed so that I could finally speak with Javier.

I was talking to him.

He couldn't hear me.

His techno music sealed him off from the world and from me.

The sections of Paris, the ones I passed through on that cold and wet night, did not, fortunately, give up on me. They heard me.

Paris, at last, was with me all the way.

We were supposed to be on the same flight from Marrakech, do you remember that? We were going to travel together, maybe even sit together. Up in the sky, just you and me.

At the airport, you were with your camera buddies, the guys right under the director. You were all laughing. You all had something in common.

I wasn't with any of you, of course not. I wasn't one of you. I didn't want to impose. I could have. I was into feeling something else: my deception, my pain. The people at the check-in counter had just informed me that I wasn't going to board the same plane as you. Worse still, they didn't know when I could leave. I'd just have to wait; they'd do all they could to get me on another flight.

Wait around. Yes, there was nothing else to do.

I went over to tell you. You left your friends and you seemed to feel really sorry for me. We went for a little walk inside the main terminal. The departure hall that day looked like a souk, a marketplace full of passengers who didn't suspect what had started between us.

We walked. Didn't say much to one another. It was nice. Really, really nice.

You had to say goodbye again, your flight was leaving soon. You didn't kiss me. You held your hand out. I did the same thing. It felt strange. But I told myself your friends couldn't have been that far away from us and so, it was better to be discreet. We said goodbye like real men do, didn't we… You said, "I'll call you… back in Paris." I said, "Have a safe trip, *sahbi*!" You knew that word, *sahbi*, Arabic for "my friend." I had taught it to you, the night we made love. You smiled. It was nice. I smiled too.

You disappeared quickly. I was waiting alone, thinking of you making your way through customs, walking through the departure lounge, looking for your seat inside the aircraft, finding a place for all of your things. You told me you had a window seat. I pictured you watching Marrakech fade off into the distance, but I couldn't begin to guess how you felt about this departure, this take off for another familiar place, a place where I did not yet exist. Were you afraid? Did you think about me, even a little?

I was alone in the airport. Nearly the entire crew was booked on the same flight as you. I wanted to get out of there quickly, leave Morocco and its sun, leave Marrakech and its exoticism. Be instantly back in Paris, the city we had in common from the beginning, which we'd never spoken of.

I was stuck there for six hours.

The only thing I could think about was you.

I'd only known you for a week. I had just made love to you. The world, through my fear, my emotion, uncontrollable as I was, could be summed up in one word: You.

I was obsessed. With you. I didn't fight it, didn't resist the love story that my mind played out at breakneck speed whether you were with me or not.

They found me a seat on a flight from Agadir to Paris that would stop in Marrakech. I was saved. Or so I thought.

The plane was packed with middle-class French people who obviously knew one another. They were on their way back from a two-week stay in Agadir. There was only one empty seat. Mine. Originally, the plane wasn't supposed to stop in Marrakech. It only did because of me. It didn't take the passengers long to let me know. These French people, the kind I never ran into in Paris, people from another France, were completely foreign to me and all of them looked at me with anger in their eyes the moment I stepped aboard. I was the one who caused them the delay. They didn't like me. They wouldn't talk to me. They wouldn't do anything to rescue me. And I couldn't help myself, I was paranoid again. I could see what they were thinking: A Moroccan in the middle of a planeload of French people! I had no business being here. I just put my head down and took my seat.

Silence before takeoff.

The sky was blue. The afternoon sun was mild and caressing.

The plane took off.

It climbed into the sky, headed for the clouds. I clutched my seat, like I usually do, and waited for the terrible and exciting moment to be over. I closed my eyes and locked my knees together.

I wasn't thinking about anything. I was somewhere between fear and a big panic attack, here, but in an abstract way. My head was empty, everything turning dark.

Suddenly, we dropped. You would have thought that the plane had run into an invisible wall, an imaginary tower. That it was going to explode at any second. And before it did, we fell, dropping down in a terrible and dizzying plunge. All the passengers screamed. I could feel my heart jump out of my chest. I was scared to death and that wasn't the half of it. My whole body went numb. I was in total shock. I screamed too, of course I did.

It was the apocalypse. Death, in my face.

The plane kept dropping. Was going to break apart, disintegrate into a thousand pieces and we were too, right along with it.

Then it straightened out. And dropped again. And we all started screaming, screaming again at the top of our lungs.

It seemed as though the plane was fighting against something. But what? Nobody knew. It straightened itself out. The sky was still blue, beautiful, warm, not a cloud to be seen.

Eventually, we heard the flight attendant come on the loudspeaker. Her voice was oddly calm, but whatever she was trying to say was incomprehensible. In any case, she didn't have time to finish. Another jolt hit. We dropped, falling as far as we did the first two times. There we were, the whole plane shaking, trembling again in midair.

It made me relive my close call with death, how that high-tension surge of electricity had shot through me just as my childhood ended, had smashed me, calmly, nicely, into a thousand pieces, the only difference being that this time I didn't pass out. Some day I'll tell you the story of the first time I died. Seated inside the wild aircraft, I was convinced that I was going to die, I saw it happening, felt it happening, could feel it in the air, and there was nothing I could do about it, nothing. Just shout out my fear and my resignation, yell inside as loud as I could.

I didn't pray. That surprised me. I didn't think about my father or my mother. My entire life did not flash before my eyes. No, nothing like that happened. The only thing I heard was a voice, a voice that welled up in my mind and in my heart and kept repeating over and over, "I love you Javier... I am going to die... I love you Javier... I am going to die and I love you Javier... I love you Javier..."

My final thoughts were about you. You. Do you hear me?

Everything became crystal clear. I saw what my feelings for you really were about. I no longer had anything to lose, anything else to live for. I finally admitted to myself that I loved you, had loved you right from the start, but hadn't been able to face that fact, until then.

I was on my way out. Up in the sky, headed for another world. This was it. Total terror. Total tears. Totally convinced my number was up. Unsure about the afterlife. Unsure about this love, this love I finally declared. Finally recognized.

No, Javier, I didn't pray. The plane didn't crash. A miracle happened. After five minutes of sheer hell, the pilot managed to regain control of the aircraft.

Everyone on board let out a huge sight of relief. A lot of them kept crying, sobbing louder than before. Obviously no one thought about stopping them.

The flight attendants reappeared. Their faces were as pale as our own. They didn't speak. They comforted us in silence.

In silence.

No one dared to speak, for fear of angering something unknown… several passengers sat moving their lips in prayer. Fear was still flying with us in the cabin.

As for me, I felt an overwhelming urge to vomit. I stood up and nearly ran to the back of the plane where the bathrooms were. The few passengers who saw me must have thought I was crazy or possessed.

I was to blame for everything we had just experienced.

I spent almost half an hour throwing up in the bathroom. And praying, finally praying. For myself. For that plane. For love that in blindness had stumbled upon me. Praying for you. Of course, for you.

I was sick. Really sick.

Belleville was asleep.

I walked home along Simon-Bolivar Boulevard.

I was almost there. It was raining harder. I was soaked down to the bone. I wasn't shivering. I wasn't cold. I had turned into a zombie. A crazy man walking at night. A mystic consumed by love.

A love that was rejected.

The minute I set foot in my small apartment, an apartment that offered a view of the vast skies of Paris, I wrote a short text message and sent it to Javier.

JAVIER, HELLO! I THINK, NO, I'M ABSOLUTELY CONVINCED, THAT I'M IN LOVE WITH YOU. I WANT TO KNOW HOW YOU FEEL ABOUT ME. I NEED TO KNOW, RIGHT NOW... ABDELLAH

The following morning, there were two text messages on my cell phone.

Text message #1 at 1:30 a.m.

ABDELLAH, I ONLY WISH I FELT THE SAME WAY YOU
DID... SORRY, MY FRIEND... HUGS, JAVIER

Text message #2 at 2:10 p.m.

CAN'T WE BE FRIENDS, JUST FRIENDS? HUGS, JAVIER

I had a fever. I took two Tylenols. I was in bed for a week.
Plunged into a staggering void. I didn't panic. I didn't cry. I
kept track of the days. The nights.

I had to get out of bed. Cairo was waiting for me. I had
to set things up so we could start filming a little movie I'd
been working on for quite some time. Before I had met Javier,
I used to think I'd be happy by the time I arrived back in
Cairo. Things had changed in the meantime. Didn't work out
as planned. Not like I hoped for.

I never answered Javier's two messages, those texts full
of hugs.

I had nothing else to say.

III

RUNNING AWAY

I needed to talk to someone, confide in someone, confess everything. I needed to find a sympathetic ear. I was afraid. Afraid again. I was on the plane headed to Cairo. Everything was going fine, but I was afraid, still afraid. I really needed to talk, to babble on about something. I needed to forget. Forget about my problems. I could have made small talk with the old skeleton of a woman—no doubt an Arab—in the seat next to me. But she had fallen asleep the minute the plane took off. Was she afraid too? Had she taken a tranquilizer or sleeping pill so she'd doze off quickly without subjecting her fragile body to the panic-producing movements of the machine? Probably. She was probably just like me. Overcome with anxiety. A troubled soul. A sister. I leaned in closer. Our arms touched. I could smell her perfume, a typically eastern blend. She was my mother. She was a complete stranger. A female relative of mine. That's how it was, I had decided it that way, strongly. I closed my eyes gently and in my mind, started a conversation with her. I was dreaming with her of my body. The short-lived tale of my body. She was listening to me. She understood. She knew. And every once in a while, she'd make a little snoring sound, a sound that never woke her up, that never interrupted the telling of my tale, never brought my daydream to a close. There we were, my body and hers, suspended.

Certain women in Hay Salam would sometimes stop me on the street, moved to pity, asking me as they ran their hands down my face, "What's wrong with you, child? Why are you so thin? Why, you're nothing but skin and bones... don't you eat? Don't they feed you at home? Don't your parents have enough money for food? You have to do something, you're so thin... too thin..."

They thought I was sick and they were right. They behaved like surrogate mothers, worried mothers. There was something about me, something odd, something that touched them. I wasn't part of this world anymore. I didn't remember I had a body. I weighed 110 lbs. I was just wasting away, more and more. I went from being a loud-mouthed, effeminate street kid who liked to fight to a very silent, young 20-year-old man. They were on to me. They wanted to save me from despair, keep me from the dark. They walked towards me and every time they did, I was moved. They gazed at me with loving kindness, bestowed their blessing, their *baraka*.

So, human beings hadn't forgotten about me completely, even though all I wanted to do was disappear, become invisible, fade into silence and not have to answer the world's questions, vanish without having to make any sense of life, find the hidden meaning in the years that lay ahead, years that made no promises, offered no certainty, no joy, a life where I'd get by, accept things the way they were, accept my life as it ground to a halt, get by on unemployment like all my friends in Hay Salam, dream all my dreams alone and that would be that, me dreaming alone, alone, dreaming as I'd always done since childhood. I did exist, I did. I existed for those traditional women, women who could be strong when they had to be, women who, like me, had been incarcerated by rules despite themselves. I wasn't dead. I just didn't know how to live anymore, didn't know how to get through my days and my nights with the intensity life required. I had forgotten all about my body. I ate almost nothing. I was very thin and that's how I stayed. For a long time.

My dream continued in the sky. I had so many things to talk about, things I wanted to share, and I didn't feel shy around the old woman. I blabbed my big, long tale in just a few short words. The futility that saved me. The roller coaster ride of all my emotions.

When I arrived in Paris in 1998, I still weighed 120 lbs.

Five years later, in 2003, I was extremely frightened when I discovered on the night of my birthday that my weight had shot up, it was well over 150 lbs. Worse than that, I was just one pound away from 155 lbs!

I took off all my clothes. I stood in front of a little mirror that I keep in the bathroom, the one I used to check out every last detail of my body. I dragged a chair in and climbed up on it.

It was two o'clock in the morning.

I was looking at myself stark naked. The face that looked back at me was a different face, the body I saw, a different body, a very different body. The body was a far cry from the way I pictured myself in my mind, nothing like how Abdellah thought about himself on the inside. Something about me had changed, something inside me, and I didn't even realize it had happened. Time had taken its toll. People used to say I looked so young and now, here it was, a whole new reality staring at me in the face: I was old and I was starting to get fat. Me, fat! I was past my prime, starting with my body.

Ho-ly shit! Double holy shit. Old and fat!

This time, I was the one who told myself, "Hey, you have to do something, you have to do something fast!"

Had to get back to the old me, the thin me. The way I looked before. Had to get some of the old Abdellah back, some of the guy back who arrived in Paris ecstatic and deceived, just taking it all in. I had to get him back, find him again, find him before he disappeared, disappeared forever.

Still standing on the chair, standing naked in the middle of the night, I tried to remember what the old Abdellah had looked like. How he had looked when he first arrived in the city of his dreams. He must have been smiling. Couldn't help but smile because he had made it, was finally there, happy to see that the dream he had for so long was finally coming true. But no, that's not how it was. Abdellah back then did a lot of writing and a lot of crying, writing and crying. France wasn't all it was supposed to be. Every day, he was in for another let-down. Disappointment had to happen. He was expecting an entirely different experience. A different set of days. And then came a surprise: He never dreamed he'd become a writer. Paris gave him writing as a gift, bestowed it on him. It changed his destiny. That's how he'd start, he'd start with writing and then, by using French words, by using literature itself, he'd work his way towards writing for the movies, yes the movies, the movies, with all their haunting images.

He wasn't smiling. He was already writing, writing like a man possessed, a man whose madness came from his mother, from his country. He spoke with his *jinns*, begged them to help him survive, to find the courage to live differently in reality, without the sunshine of the Parisian hours. He was still thin, but didn't realize it mattered to him. He would cry. Cry because he was happy. Because he was afraid. Because he was heartbroken. Cry over Paris itself. Because he was there, not far from Marcel Proust's grave. Cry because he had left Morocco, left its crowds, left his childhood, left them there, off in the distance.

I could see Abdellah. Naive. In love. Lazy. Ambitious. Determined to make it somehow in Paris. Impatient. Bad news for anyone who fell in love with him. He was alone and happier than ever to be that way. All alone and sadder than ever because of it.

I could see him, picture him very clearly.

Yes, that was me, the me of fiction, the me of reality.

But that wasn't me anymore.

I'd put on another 35 lbs. I was 5 years older. Had a fat stomach, a puffed-out face. I wasn't so young looking. My dream of making movies was still nothing but a dream.

The mirror pointed things out. No beating around the bush and no pity.

What I saw was what I looked like. In reality. That was my body.

I had to make some changes, change the way it looked.

I had to get my old body back, the one I had the day I left, the day I arrived.

Yes, I had to lose weight. Seriously lose weight.

Just stop eating.

Gamble with death, gamble once again without even knowing it.

Made in Egypt. I really liked the title of the movie. And more than the title, I loved what the film was about. A guy who was looking for his father. The director had already filmed a lot of the story in France. He still had to shoot some scenes in Cairo. In order to do that, he needed me to be there, both as his interpreter and his assistant.

Karim Goury never saw his father. He was brought up by his French mother and she did everything she could to keep the father figure away from her children and their world. She had her reasons. Her regrets. Her battles.

Karim is a tall guy who's the same age as me. He's good-looking, light-skinned, completely French in every way. When I first met him, his whole Egyptian look struck me immediately. Here was the son of the Nile raised miles away from the river. A man of the East trying to find out who he was. A courageous and moving young man who, after his mother dies, decides with camera in hand, to go looking for his father. See him. Touch him. See himself reflected in him. Talk to him.

His father had also died, passed away a long time ago.

Karim was sophisticated. He might have been very strong, no doubt very strong, but he was going down, he was going to lose it. He was starting to cry. Real tears, nothing pathetic. He acted like a man, vulnerable and reinvented and that was beautiful to watch. He walked around like his mind was made up, walked around like he was not sure, and all you wanted to do was follow him. He was feeling his way through his dark Egyptian past and like my mother, I wanted to give him all my prayers and my full support, my help from far away and from up close. I wanted to become his brother, his interpreter, his voice in the Arabic language.

His father left behind a legend, a reputation that both fascinated and frightened Karim as he tried to discover the truth behind it, to understand it. A few fingerprints, some long and beautiful letters, audio recordings, photographs, articles of clothing that were never washed after the man had worn them, an apartment in Héliopolis, loyal friends who were never reluctant to reinvent his life, so that every retelling made him sound even more wonderful. Most importantly, this man who looked like Omar Sharif left quite a family behind, a big, complicated family, which Karim knew nothing about. Aunts. Cousins. Half-brothers. Half-sisters. With their help, Karim would try to picture his father the way he really was. That was what the whole movie was about. A way to stop focusing on the images created by his mother and instead, come face to face with his father on his own, directly.

Karim was going through a lot of changes. Happy, then unhappy. I was with him the entire week in Cairo, at his side while he went through internal shifts. He was very good about it, he let me watch it all happen. Be part of it. Observe it in silence. And my own father, my savior, the man who had brought me back to life after my electrocution, he was there, he was there too. He had died in 1996. Now he was alive. Still alive in Cairo, there for the first time.

The three-star hotel we stayed in was absolutely filthy. But it didn't matter.

I was exploring Cairo again, back in the heart of the Arab world. I was rediscovering the gigantic, insane city where I had spent two happy and complicated months in 2002, a city I thought I'd never see again. That was what was important. A chance to run away, lose myself in my love for this generous city.

Sabah was making a comeback. The Lebanese singer of mythical legend, the woman well into her 80s had, thanks to face-lifts, transformed herself into a statue, a mummy, an icon, a strange-looking young girl with very blond hair that billowed out and wildly away. She had become a woman with a slightly raucous voice, a performer who defied both time and the Arab world. People thought that she had died. But she wasn't completely dead. She was back on the hit parade, back on the charts with her song, "Yana Yana," a song I often listened to as a child. People were playing it again and the remixed version she performed with another Lebanese diva became the hit song of the season. Cairo, as always, was a trendsetter, and what caught on in Cairo eventually spread to the rest of the Arab world.

"Yana Yana" was everywhere. "Yana Yana," happy and sad. It played in cars, cafés, stores, snack bars and it was already being sold as a ring tone for cell phones. People couldn't help but notice it. It worked its way inside our heads as we tried to finish this movie about a father. After hearing it day after day, I thought of it as a soundtrack, the theme song that went along with our quest, the music behind our project. I learned the words very quickly and I'd hum along, constantly hum along, with the music video they kept showing on Muzzika, Melody Hits, Rotana Clips, and all the music stations I'd watch in my hotel room at night, stations that in the last few years had invaded the Arab countries. The clip made Sabah look blonder and more like a fossil than ever. Miraculously, her voice hadn't changed, but her face, her face had become a mask, perhaps death's own mask. Sabah was back, back from the dead, back to delight the Arabs, delight them and make them dance. Make them forget, if only for a little while, the sadness that often hits as the year draws to a close. But this comeback event, it was kind of sad to begin with, a sad event in and of itself. Sabah wasn't Sabah anymore. The golden age of movies and music, those years I knew so well, years where she had contributed so very much, they all came to a close, ending at least three decades ago. Oum Kalthoum, Abdelhalim Hafez, Farid El Atrach, Ismahan, Mohammed

Abdelwahhab, all the giants in the world of Egyptian music, artists everybody in the Arab world knew and loved, they were all dead now, had died a long time ago. Sabah was a survivor. A yellow corpse that filled you with fear and filled you with pleasure, both at the same time.

Karim and the director of photography had never heard of her. I tried explaining who she was, tried listing all her accomplishments, retelling the myth that surrounded her. No interest whatsoever. Sabah did nothing for them and they thought that "Yana, Yana" was stupid, a low-budget waste of time. I didn't make a big deal of it. The fact that they didn't get it—I didn't want that to ruin Sabah's return to life, to tint my return to Cairo with sadder and sadder colors.

The filming lasted one week.

First, Karim filmed one part of his Egyptian family and found the experience incredibly moving. There was a rich, rather eccentric aunt who lived in a hotel suite for half the year. And a cousin, an engineer, who was short and a little on the heavy side, so overwhelmed with work that his cell phone never stopped ringing. Another aunt, a divorced, devout Muslim who wore a veil, stayed up all night, slept all day and cancelled our meeting at the last minute because all of a sudden she was afraid that the film might cast Islam in an unfavorable light by displaying Karim's father's penchant for women and poker, which she deemed out of control and immature.

Of all the people we met that week, it was Héba his half-sister who impressed me the most. I admit that in a certain way, I fell in love with her, kind of.

In an Egyptian society that veiled its women more and more, Héba was a free woman, someone who lived her life with sincerity and conviction. She was as beautiful as any movie star, on par with Mervat Amine who made so many of the movies I enjoyed watching, especially romantic comedies. Héba had a graceful way of smoking, an elegance that wasn't provocative. She always wore black, a color that made her silhouette even more charming. When she walked down the street, you couldn't help but notice how people looked at her, standing there surprised as if she were the last surviving representative of a species headed for extinction. Men were captivated by her, couldn't take their eyes off her, but none of them dared show her anything but respect. She'd walk by and everybody had the same question. Who is that? She was a star. And not just in my mind. She was a mystery woman, a woman with a hint of sadness in her eyes. She was an exceptional human being, a woman who could easily provide the inspiration for a movie you wanted to make, a novel you planned to write, or a poetry collection you had in mind.

And here she was in our midst, a woman who resonated strength and sweetness, even in her silence, without a hint of embarrassment. So alive, right in front of us.

Karim filmed her reading some letters she had written back when she was a teenager, letters she wrote to her father, a man with whom she had always had a difficult relationship, a man who, most of the time, was missing from her life. They were loving letters, long and full of blame, letters that gave her a way to tell him in simple and precise language how bad it was not having him around, that gave her a way to settle the score, a way to cry, to pray. Héba read them in a clear, easy to understand voice, a voice that covered up her emotions. Sometimes, though, her emotions got the best of her. You would watch her eyes well up with tears, watch her cheeks take on a reddish color. Karim would stop filming. Héba didn't move. We didn't either. She put her head down. A few minutes later, she looked up again. She had a calm look on her face, but deep down, she must have been upset.

I liked what I saw. I liked the fact that my job as an interpreter allowed me to witness and be part of the whole experience. I liked being in the room while Héba revealed her true feelings and at the same time, hid them. I liked being in the presence of a woman who forgot nothing about her past and all the ways it hurt her, a woman who had not yet moved on with her life and stayed in the pain, right in front of us, simple, sad, without a hint of deception. She was dignified. And beautiful. Beautiful.

The second round of filming focused on places associated with Karim's father: a café with a bar in the Hélipolis part of the city, the building where he spent the final years of his life, the streets he knew, his barber, his tomb inside the immense and fascinating City of the Dead. And last but not least, the mythical hotel at the foot of the Pyramids at Giza, the hotel where Karim's father and mother met. Karim had an old black and white photograph that captured the moment forever. He managed to find the room where the picture was taken and even found the same angle. He filmed the exact location, an empty, full space, filmed it a long time, filmed it all alone. He spent an entire day filming it. Then an entire night. He couldn't calm down.

I was there that day, but he didn't need an interpreter so I just watched him, kept my distance and watched.

On day four, something extraordinary happened, at least I thought it was extraordinary. I met Karabiino. He was working at our hotel, cleaning rooms.

Dark. Very dark.

Blue. Dressed exclusively in blue. A deep blue, a blue that in some strange way, seemed to blend right into the color of his skin.

A surprising body, long. Thin but powerful. Strong.

He moved with the lightness of a leaping gazelle.

Seeing him was a whole new experience for me. He had a presence about him, filled the entire room, every single corner. The minute he'd show up to clean the room, all I could do was look at him, look at him right in front of me, alive and in the flesh. I watched him breathe. Watched him walk. I watched him bend down and stand up again. Watched him use the broom. Fold the blankets. Clean the floor, the sink, the bathtub. Change the towels.

I hadn't done a lot of traveling at that point in my life.

When I met Karabiino, I realized that humanity was a species I hardly knew anything about. This boy was not like me. We couldn't have come from the same background. Shared the same roots. That would have been impossible. I knew that, of course, but I couldn't stop noticing that fact and repeating it over and over again to myself. After all, I was an African too, just like him. He seemed so innocent, so unjaded, still very sweet, untouched by the banality that you find in other men.

This 17-year-old kid completely changed my definition of what it meant to be a man and at the same time, revolutionized my concept of what it meant to be charming.

I didn't miss any of his moves, glued to his side.

It was morning. Early. I still had an hour to spare before I had to meet Karim and the cameraman and head out to the City of the Dead.

A whole hour all to myself. A little moment of eternity when I could admire and love Karabiino.

Talk to him. Talk in Arabic.

Karabiino was a Christian and came from Darfur. Along with an older brother, he had fled death after he watched Sudanese Arab guerrilla fighters kill his father and mother with a machete. He saw their heads. Just the heads. No bodies. The image haunted him, would always haunt him. He and his brother didn't have time to give his parents a proper burial or put together any kind of service. They had to get out of there and get out fast. Had to save their own skin.

They had to wander for months and months in the desert. Beg for food in villages. Sometimes, they had to steal. And sometimes they'd die and then be brought back to life. Manage somehow. Manage to stay alive. Find some way to make it into Egypt. Walk and walk and just keep on walking, walk the whole length of the Nile. Head north. Head towards Cairo. Towards the great city. Walk, walk, into their own exile. Walk towards hope itself. Towards hell.

He'd been living in the Egyptian capital for about a year. He lived with his brother, shared a rooftop near Al-Ataba Square. He didn't want to stay in Cairo. He didn't like Egyptians. "They're racist," he said. "Racist. When I walk down the street, they call me names because I'm black... And then they throw rocks at me... I can't say anything... I can't even fight back, because they're liable to throw me in jail and start torturing me, torturing me for no reason at all. I don't have any papers here... I'm an illegal alien. I live on the sly." He didn't cry when he told me all this. He wasn't a baby about it, even if he hadn't been a man for very long. He didn't cry about things anymore. He just put up with them. Kept on working. And not for much. But he had his big dream: to go to Australia. It was a place where a man could be free, miles and miles away from these lousy people and this hellhole brimming with negativity and despair. Freedom, that's what he was looking for, freedom. In a few days, he'd try to earn that freedom by filing a request for asylum with the Australian Embassy. "It's going to work out... I'm going to make it... It's all going to work out..." He kept repeating the words, saying them over and over again, quietly, as if they were a kind of prayer. And that was it, his big plan, his dream, the whole reason he went on living, which he shared with me, shared at that very moment. With me, the Arab who was part white, the foreigner who lived in Paris.

I was ashamed of myself around him. I felt old, blasé. But I was there, alongside him, and I understood everything he was hoping for and all the things he hoped would never happen. Yes, he was in a bad situation, but he was miraculously fresh. He held his head up high, regardless of stones and insults. His faith was strong. He spoke of Christ with love and admiration. That was his one great blessing, the light still shining inside him.

I liked him a lot.

I felt like I wanted to touch him. Not to make love. I just wanted to touch somebody who was like me and, at the same time, who was very different. Only touch Karabiino, touch him like a brother. Touch him so I could share who knows what of myself with him and in return, receive just a portion of who knows what from him, a being from the elemental world, a being who was almost an ancestor. An adolescent fighting to make it. A person so full of grace. Despite everything. Grace in his eyes. Grace on his black skin.

And then I did it.

I got up. I walked over to him and without saying a word, reached out to touch his face. I put my hand on his forehead and left it there. I closed my eyes.

Karabiino did the same thing.

I felt the warmth and softness of his hand against my forehead. A whisper and a prayer issued from his mouth. I felt the angel that he was enter my very being.

He gave me more than I gave him.

He understood that we were brothers.

He knew what I was about. Knew just how to answer me. It didn't surprise me, not in the least.

We stayed like that for a long time.

I saw Karabiino again the following morning. Not for long. I had only fifteen minutes, that was it. I had to leave, be on my way to film Karim's sister. He was all in blue, just like yesterday, except the shoes were different. He had on green espadrilles, simple, very pretty. I loved them at once, wanted a pair for myself. I told him that. He stopped cleaning for a minute and explained where I could find them: Al-Ataba, Al-Ataba Square, near downtown. I knew the place, a gigantic, quite interesting intersection. He was kind, very touching, and in a high-pitched voice that spoke an Arabic I'd never heard before, he went on to say, "They're not expensive... not expensive at all... You'll see... But they only come in green, no other colors." I was very moved by all this attention on his part. I wanted a pair of the espadrilles, a pair just like his.

I still had five minutes left.

I put the TV on. Melody Hits was showing the video version of Sabah's song. Karabiino knew the song but he didn't know anything about the artist. He stopped working.

I invited him to come sit next to me on the bed. We watched the video together. It was so happy. And so sad. Overwhelming. Unlike anything else. There was Sabah, defying death, defying time, standing once again and forever more, Sabah waging her final battle. Suddenly, I felt like crying without knowing why and Karabiino just sat there, eyes glued to the screen. Was he happy? Did he manage to forget all his troubles, even for a moment? What was he thinking about? Who was he, what was he really like? I couldn't answer that. I didn't have to. Karabiino was a boy who simply showed up one day, in my room and in my memory, a boy I understood perfectly well, a boy who remained a perfect mystery. I knew part of his saga, part of his dream. But sitting next to me, he was like a little prince, a little king. A little sphinx. Elusive. Somewhere off in the distance. Always beyond reach.

It was time to go. I headed downstairs to meet Karim and the cameraman. Sabah was still singing. I jumped up and went into the bathroom. I took my bottle of "Ambre Sultan" and gave it to Karabiino.

"I am this fragrance. So with this perfume, I'm giving a little bit of myself to you... Please accept it. Keep it a long time. It's called 'Ambre Sultan.' I'm sure it's going to be fabulous on your skin... Don't throw it away, even when the bottle is empty, keep it..."

He smiled.

It was sad. Very sad.

He knew what was happening.

We'd never see one another again.

He stood up too and said, "I'll bring it with me to Australia." He walked over to me and for three or four seconds placed his hand on my forehead.

I closed my eyes and inhaled deeply.

When I left the room, Sabah had just finished singing "Yana Yana."

Apparently, I wasn't over Javier yet. But I had made a decision: To rid myself of him. Get him out of my mind and my memory. Get all his poison out of my system. Destroy all the beautiful images I built around him in my mind. Not make myself sick over him anymore.

Well, it's easy to talk about, easy to plan. But doing it, of course that's the hard part.

How do you walk away from love? Away from its insanity? How could I steer the machine of my emotions, the vehicle that had driven off with me before I even knew it? What about the taste in my mouth, the one I associated with Javier, with his body, with whatever it was that still reminded me of his smell? How are you supposed to go on living when you're totally entangled in the sad, bitter, exciting memory of someone who didn't love you back?

I had my job. Fortunately. Work, work, work, from morning to night. Another tale of obsession. Karim as part of his father's past, a past that still was very much alive. The images he came up with. The endless traveling. The doubt. The way reality was reconstructed. All the preparation. All the phone calls so we could have the authorization at the last minute to do such and such. The film we needed to finish. The certain feeling Karim was hoping to recapture, hoping somehow to control.

And then there was my obsession with losing weight. Weight loss as a way to distance myself from Javier, to destroy the body that he once touched, to go back to being the old Abdellah, the Abdellah he never knew. To keep losing weight, even in Cairo. To get back to what I weighed before, less than 120 lbs. To start over again. Take a good look at myself. Yes, I was over 30. I hadn't forgotten.

And there was Cairo, Cairo the chaotic, Cairo the city that fit me like a glove.

Cairo. Al-Qahira. A Turkish bathhouse with 20 million bathers. A human monster. A blue flower, beautiful and covered with dust. An inspiring, stifling desert. A film by Youssef Chahine, *Cairo Station*. A song by Abdelhalim Hafez, "Ana Lak Aala Toul."

> *I am yours forever.*
> *Stay here with me.*
> *Take one of my eyes,*
> *And come back to look at me.*
> *Take both my eyes,*
> *And come back to see how I'm doing.*
> *From the first day I met you,*
> *I haven't been able to sleep.*

The night after Karim and the cameraman left, I was all alone in Cairo, and I had a dream about my brother and how he came to meet God. I must have been 15 and he was 11 or 12. I was no longer my mother's favorite. Now it was Mustapha who slept beside her during the afternoon siesta. He had taken over my spot. No matter how hard I tried, I was still very jealous. And more than that, Mustapha was as a matter of course, overprotected, defended and pardoned. He didn't like school very much and instead of making him go, my mother let him stay home, keeping him for herself. In those days, Mustapha, more than anyone else in the family, received every advantage my mother's prayers, protection and blessings could offer. My mother claimed he was *chrif*, that there was something saintly about him. He wasn't like the rest of us.

Those were the years when I started calling my mother by her first name, M'Barka, instead of mom.

It happened one Sunday. It was winter. I remember it very

clearly. We were sitting eating breakfast. Bread, olive oil, mint tea, same as always. M'Barka had decided that Mustapha could sleep late. The family was eating in silence. Ten of us, sitting around a small, low table. Mustapha was still off in dreamland sleeping on my mother's bed.

All of a sudden, he was standing, shaking, shaking and crying his eyes out. His teeth were chattering and then he blurted out, "I saw God... I saw God... I swear, I saw God in one of my dreams." He collapsed, maybe fainted. Maybe he was... dead? But no, no, he kept talking, talking in a strange voice that none of us had ever heard before. "I am with you... with you... I am God..." M'Barka screamed, "My son! My son!" She got up and threw herself across him, sobbing and sobbing. "My son... My son... Please don't die. I love you, sweetie, I love you... Stay here with us, stay here with us... Oh God, please, please don't take him... God, he's still so young... Still my little baby..." Not only was Mustapha not dead, but he had been granted his very own miracle. God had revealed Himself to him.

He opened his eyes. My mother immediately put her arms around him. The rest us, in total disbelief, moved in closer. Three of my sisters were crying. My father read from the Koran. Mustapha, the newest prophet, carried on acting out his delirium and theatrics. We believed him, so why would he have stopped? "I met God... He came to me. God spoke to me..." That's when M'Barka asked him the big, important question that was on everybody's mind. "Well, what does God look like?" Mustapha looked at her for a minute, and then he started crying and told her, "He's handsome… Tall… He has a beard." That's all he had to say.

My mother was ecstatic. Her darling little boy was undoubtedly special. She wouldn't stop kissing him and holding him close to her, very close to her. You would have thought they were making love. They didn't even notice the rest of us, paid us no mind. We were just nobodies, members of the family passed over by God.

From that day on, Mustapha enjoyed every privilege you could imagine. He could do anything he wanted. Act like a spoiled brat from sunup to sundown. Quit school. Waste his life away. You couldn't say a thing to him, you couldn't blame him for anything. He had become a saint. Though he knew what glory was, he soon would meet his downfall. For God did not reveal Himself a second time in his dreams. Mustapha wound up forfeiting his exalted title and lost all his privileges. His usurping was over. His God had given up on him. Like we all did, in the end.

As for me, I was jealous, I was angry, I became a heathen, and from that day on, I seriously doubted the existence of God. I had my doubts about Him and about everybody else.

In Cairo, after Karim left, doubt turned into conviction.

God had given up on me and I had given up on Him. On the other hand, I always needed people to pray for me.

But who exactly were they supposed to pray to?

I spent three days by myself in Cairo. By myself in the crowds. Swept along. Knocked over. Crushed. Just another madman in a sea of crazies. Haunted more and more by a phantom Javier.

His spirit had left me alone while we were filming. But now that it was just the two of us, his ghost and me, the spirit went back to being a distant master, the master who ordained that I should suffer, that every day I lived would bring nothing more than heartbreak. I was possessed by him. Rendered miserable by him. In love with him. Was beginning to fall out of love with him. I had no idea how long it might take me to rout him from my imagination, to find some way that my body and my mind could negotiate with him and all his different ghosts.

The reality of my unfortunate love for Javier hit me again. More and more, I wasn't a man who controlled my own heart. It stopped beating for me, stopped working to keep me alive. My head, my overheated head. I thought it was going to explode at any minute. Not from some kind of fever. It was caught in a gigantic inferno.

I had left the hotel, moved into a big apartment, a place that belonged to another era, a place in the very beautiful and poetically named neighborhood, Garden City. It belonged to a friend of mine, Pierre, who had taught at the French School for more than twenty years and had gone back to Paris to celebrate New Year's. The apartment was where I spent a good part of my first day alone, going up to the faucet every once in a while and sticking my head under it. Nice cold water, water to let me forget, let me breathe differently, let me appease Javier's many spirits, and I was really hoping, water to let me be cured, start to feel better, at least a little bit better.

Javier was ever present in my body, on my skin, living the life that should have been mine to live. I no longer knew what he wanted from me. I no longer knew what I wanted from him.

I wasn't myself anymore.

I had to rediscover who I was. That's why I left the apartment, to lose myself in the streets of Cairo.

I didn't know that doing so would only make things worse.

I didn't know that it would mark the end of all faith. Make me a man with no religion. A man without God. A man thrown into the void and vertigo. A man distraught in the labyrinth that is Cairo. A place of madness. A place of collapse. I was in the heart of the Arab world, a world that when you came down to it, no longer believed in anything either. An absurd world. A prison of a world where starting now, poetry would become a rare thing. A world that never tired of making the same mistakes over and over again, and blaming someone else each and every time. The West, the West, it was all their fault! I had no more leniency when it came to the Arab world. No soft spot left. None for Arabs and none for myself. I suddenly saw things with merciless lucidity. With real horror. I was losing it. The Arab world was losing it even faster than I was. Going to pieces along with me. We were in perfect harmony, but that was only on the surface. We had lost our head for a while, and it was now hope that was leaving us, emigrating from us. We were both falling, caught in the CRY and in the nostalgia. The nostalgia of ignorance.

Nothing would ever be the same again. God no longer existed, that's what I really believed. I was going to hell. I was damned. Damned.

I wandered around.

What did I have left?

One happy memory, a memory that turned happy as time went on, a memory of a love that wasn't love, that had been love at times. A memory of an Algerian named Slimane, the man I lived with four years ago, the man who once played such a great part in a long, passionate relationship. Slimane, who was madly in love with me, Slimane, the ghost I found so miraculously soothing in Cairo. Cairo, where we had dreamed of going. I was in Cairo. Without him.

What did I have left?

Same as always, tombs, mausoleums, saints.

I was caught up in the horror of my own state of confusion. I could see that confusion. Understand it perfectly. Wherever I went, my confusion went with me, sometimes in silence, sometimes fighting all the way, but it never gave me a single minute of peace. I was powerless, under the control of a force greater than myself, an invisible, unknown power that was pushing me towards my own private chaos.

There were times when I could see my sister Lattéfa in myself, Lattéfa, the girl people said was possessed. Who was possessed. I'd see images of her body suddenly being taken over by someone else. Someone you couldn't see, but you'd clearly hear a voice, a voice that came from the world beyond this one. Lattéfa would cease to exist. Her body would lose its shape and all its sense of gravity. She'd fall down, quickly of course. And then she'd roll around, like a sheep that just had its throat slit. She'd flash her genitals, exhibit what we weren't supposed to see. Explode before our eyes, dumbfounded.

Lattéfa was possessed but I never understood how it had started for her. How was she to blame? I mean, what crime did she ever commit? What was the point of it all? How long was she supposed to live like that, out of touch with herself, living like a stranger who was one step away from madness?

I was Lattéfa. And like her, I went to visit a saint, the nearest one I could find. The saint was Sayyéda Zeinab, the most important saint in Egypt, the one whose mausoleum was not far from Garden City. Her tomb was impressive and the fervor of her followers was magnificent to see, to listen to. They came from everywhere, dressed as if they were going to a wedding. They dressed up to visit the Lady of Cairo, the city's patron saint, the daughter of the Prophet Mohammed. They would sing her prayers, prayers they had just invented, whispering mystical poems to her, drawing near to her, huddling against her tomb, touching the large, exquisite green cloth that covered it, touching it and weeping. Men, women, children, old people, women in veils, women in too much makeup, men with mustaches, men with beards, poor people, very rich people, Muslims, Copts, dwarfs, unhappy people, newlyweds, drug addicts, Blacks, whites, those who had made a fortune in oil... A dense crowd, a single unit welded together across all social lines, a crowd joined as one in the unorthodox expression of their unique love. An over-flowing crowd, one that cried out, louder and louder. Cried out in ecstasy. Cried out as the tenets of their sensuous, sexual religion demanded, cried out as Sufis. Bodies, bodies, bodies and this exquisite scent, smoke from the precious incense they kept continuously lit. A world unto itself, an island apart, a few feet from the Nile.

I jumped into the crowd. Enraptured. A dervish full of love and misfortune. A Moroccan child living in Paris in the middle of a major crisis. Someone without roots. With a very strident conscience. I sang along with them. I danced. I shouted. I didn't know whether I believed in anything anymore, but I did know that the crowd moving around the Lady of Cairo would do me good, maybe even save me.

Caught up in the movement towards a world far beyond my own, I incessantly prayed for Lattéfa and continued to curse Javier.

I spent an entire day and a good part of the night in Sayyéda Zeinab's mausoleum.

The next day, I woke up very late. Cairo was getting ready for Friday prayers, the major event of the week. The city was calm, exceptionally calm. You could even hear the song of birds that lived in Garden City. The weather was beautiful and hot. The sky had a touch of pink, a touch of ochre. In the bathroom, I spent a good long time in the shower. I was starting to feel like myself again. My sadness was there, my skinny body. I saw that in one week's time, I'd lost some weight, that my body almost looked just like it did before. The water ran over me, warm, hot, without interruption. I sat down in the bottom of the tub. The water poured over me, flowed down stronger than before. It was rain. I was creating rain. The drops fell on my head, fell down the back of my neck, over my back, over my ass, falling onto my face, my Adam's apple, falling onto my stomach, my crotch. The water fell in fat drops, drops that hurt but felt good at the same time. I wanted to fall asleep then and there, fall asleep right under the hammering of the water, die right where I was and come back to life, come back again as a changed man, a man with a different memory, a man whose faith had been renewed, a man who could live free of Javier.

I shut off the water.

The *muezzin*, in a very beautiful voice, started to call the faithful to prayer.

I opened the window to air out the bathroom and dried myself off.

Five minutes later, a new voice, a faint, distant, marvelous, really happy, lively, dancing voice came drifting through the apartment. I recognized it immediately. It was the actress Souad Hosni singing a song called "Bambi," Egyptian Arabic for "rose." It was a song that was easy to listen to, a famous song, a romantic song, a song sung somewhere between happiness and sorrow.

I hadn't forgotten Souad Hosni. I never forgot the series she starred in, *Houa and Hiya*, a program that kept me running when I was a teenager, racing home the minute school got out. Since then, I had kept up with her by watching almost every movie she was in, I had kept track of her, close track in fact, had followed her career with a kind of admiration. Back in the early '90s, after the complete flop of her film *The 3rd Class*, she disappeared. For two or three years, nobody knew where she was. She was hiding out in London, dealing with a recurring back problem and chronic depression. People said she was flat broke, done for. In the end, the Egyptian government that had paid the bills for her hospitalization gave up on her, abandoning her completely. In June 2001, she committed suicide by jumping off the balcony of the apartment she kept in London. Even today, Egyptians don't believe her death was a suicide. In their minds, the Egyptian Secret Service killed her. Why? They can't prove it for certain, but they are convinced that the government wanted to snuff her out before she could write her memoir, a book that would have contained too many compromising secrets.

"Bambi" was still playing in the bathroom. Souad Hosni had returned. Her spirit was alive again in broad daylight, in Cairo. I linked up with her and headed down into the near-empty streets. I hailed the first cab that came along and headed out to the City of the Dead.

It took me a long time to find her grave.

Standing in front of it, I muttered prayers without even thinking. I read verses from the Koran. I said words my mother would have said.

I don't know why I went to her grave. But I do know that in the passageways of the immense and magnificent cemetery in ruins, I saw how I would end my days, leaving the earth once and for all. I saw, once again, around me, the Arab world in endless fall.

As I stood there, I wanted to cry. Sob my eyes out.

Go and throw myself off a balcony.

I needed to find someone, someone alive, in the flesh, someone real, someone visible, someone to save me. Someone to touch me. Someone to let me gaze upon him. Someone to carry me along. Someone who would make the decision for me about which path I ought to be following. Because I was now a *hayèm*, a wanderer in the desert, as in Ibn Arabi's poetry. A vagrant. A man with no direction. A man with no God.

I was walking around downtown Cairo. I wanted to buy a few small gifts for Tristan, the little 8-year-old boy I babysat. The child was like a ray of sunshine, someone who got me through the difficult days of my daily isolation back in Paris. He was a young French boy who allowed me at last to understand France, to see it from the inside, to finally get to know a French family. Tristan never let me down. The affection and closeness he felt for me were for many years my most treasured connection to humanity.

I didn't feel like I had to bring him a souvenir. But the idea of finding him one or two things was perhaps reason enough to leave the apartment in Garden City despite the panicky feeling that was growing stronger inside me. Perhaps reason enough to be around other people. Go into some stores. Do a little haggling. Pick something out. Forget about it. Keep thinking about Tristan, the sweet little kid who knew what he wanted. Talk to him in my mind.

I looked and looked and didn't find anything for him. Nothing that really caught my eye. Nothing he'd really like. Nothing he'd want to keep, hang onto forever and store in his treasure chest. That's what I was trying to do. Find him a rare and valuable gift that would remind him of Egypt forever. I didn't want just any old thing. I was hoping to luck out and find something really nice, find something nice for his sake. For my sake. For the sake of our friendship.

I wandered around for hours.

At nightfall, the panic attack finally hit. Fear was in charge from head to toe. Fear was calling all the shots.

Everything around me started to shake. The ground opened up under my feet. The abyss. I dropped into it. The cycle of blind death that I had already encountered as a child, as a young man, was starting again. I felt lost. I was lost in the desert. Lost and panicking. I was lost in the city, lost and panicking. Fear was all I felt, total panic as I felt the world slipping away. Slipping away inside me. Out from under my feet. I closed my eyes, I didn't want to see the bottom of the pit, that total nothingness, infinity. I opened my eyes. Cairo was roaring away in the high-heat atmosphere of Saturday night, indifferent to what I was going through. I needed to cry out, get somebody to help me, stop the people who walked by me and warn them, warn them that I was dying, that I was losing touch with reality, that I needed one of them to do something, something to keep me from going under, something to keep me here on earth, keep me here, here with them, something to keep me in this life. I was so afraid, so totally afraid. I was too afraid to even move.

I didn't dare.

I hugged the walls, leaned up against the fronts of buildings, and with the feeling that everything inside me was starting to explode, I slowly made my way into a little alley that was kind of dark and dirty. That's where I collapsed, simply collapsed. I didn't cry.

For the past two days, I had hardly eaten a thing. I couldn't even feel my body anymore. The inside of my mouth tasted like blood. In my brain, a revolution, a hemorrhage.

I was in death.

That's what death was like. True death. Death was imminent, the kind of death I knew was happening, the kind of death I was completely aware of.

Passing away like that, little by little, to be snuffed out with no promise of a life to come. To suddenly die. Find myself yanked out of this world, pulled right out of the human race, whisked away at top speed and in a state of total panic. No peace to be found. Not a trace of me left anywhere. Miles and miles from the place where I was born. Miles and miles away from my dreams.

Dying without bringing my images to the screen, dying without being the man behind the movie.

Dying. Dying again. Was this the third time? The fourth? Dying with my eyes open, dying without agreeing to die, dying breathing.

She was small in stature. You couldn't tell how old she was and she was dressed all in black. She was undoubtedly a beggar, but had inherited a special power. She could see what had to be done. She knew how to use the power of touch.

She was sitting next to me. She had placed her left hand on my forehead and her right hand over my heart.

She appeared, appeared out of nowhere. I hadn't seen her walk towards me.

Was she real? Did she really exist? She understood everything about me, all that I had been through, every detail of my body, every detail of my life and everything about my death.

She was whispering something, saying words in a language that seemed strangely familiar, though I couldn't understand it.

She was praying. Praying for me. Praying in a way that I couldn't. She had entered inside me, penetrated my mind, had taken over my soul, examined it with sweetness and brutality.

She smacked me, hard. Then again, just as hard. She spit into her hands and washed my face. She closed my eyes and moved her face closer to mine. Using her lips, she kissed me on the head, on the forehead and on each of my shoulders. And then, using her right hand, she pinched my nostrils shut. No more air. A very deep slumber. Darkness filled with peace. A departure with all my fears lay to rest, a departure without a bit of panic. Heading out. Out towards the distant place where a person becomes a spirit forever, an exhalation, an angel, a little devil. The place where the universe becomes your envelope, your body. Far away from the person you are now. Far from all your suffering. A place of eternal contemplation.

How much time did the whole journey take? I really don't know.

The lady in black released my nose and used her mouth to blow air all over me. Her breath, her smell and the way her body tasted entered me immediately and provoked a life-saving explosion, a violent awakening, a startling return to the world. Under the gaze of this new mother, in the city of chaos and romance, bathed and loved, I came back to life. Faith restored. Strong. Weak. Grateful.

The small woman helped me to my feet and without saying a word, invited me to walk with her through the noisy streets of Cairo. It was ten o'clock at night. The crowds were gigantic, everybody pushed together. It frightened me. I held on to the woman and together we slowly walked for quite some time until we came to Al-Ataba Square, the place where Karabiino had bought his espadrilles. I hadn't forgotten about Karabiino, the unbelievable young man. The life I led before was still there, still inside me. It would come back to me, little by little. For now, everything was all peace and angels. It was this woman, a miracle of life. Standing next to me, with me, inside me.

She had to leave, catch the subway at the station beneath the immense square.

I lovingly kissed her hands several times and then let her make her way underground.

Just before she disappeared from view, I shouted out, "What's your name?"

It took 10 seconds for the answer to reach me. I couldn't see the woman anymore.

From way down in the subway, in Arabic that was very distinctive, almost broken, she said, "Ana Yahoudiya!"

"I'm Jewish."

"Ismi Sara!"

"My name is Sara!"

Wow, what a surprise.

A Jew.

The first I had ever met.

All the things people told me about Jews, the things they crammed into my head that I had no control over, it all evaporated, vanished in a single second. All that remained was the person. This woman. Someone just like me. No different.

The realization was another miracle at the end of the trip. On an unforgettable night, on the banks of the Nile.

I stood a long time looking down into the subway entrance. And then spontaneously, I shouted out, "*Ana ismi Abdellah!*"

My flight back to Paris was scheduled to leave the next afternoon. I still had time to kill. Cairo had become a city where an important page of my life story was being written. I was well aware of that. As a way of showing my gratitude, I wanted to fully experience the expanding city, a city both miserable and humane, suffocating and poetic, a city in perpetual decline and in constant rebirth.

I walked through the streets again. Felt good as new. I felt a level of excitement I had never known before, I was so happy, felt like I had to share my happiness with everyone. Give back to the world a little of the gift which I had just received.

En route, I came across a young, barefoot young man who was selling bowls with reproductions of the Fayoum portraits on them, portraits I fell in love with the moment I discovered them in the Cairo Museum. I bought two of them. One for me and one for Tristan back in Paris.

As I was walking back, I found myself standing in front of the popular Royal El-Guidida movie theater. I didn't give it a second thought. I bought a ticket and went inside to celebrate my new life. I ended up in the middle of the big theater, the auditorium packed with men, men of all ages who were pleasuring one another with no hesitation and no shame, servicing one another only a few feet from the police officers who patrolled the entrance to the theater. There I was, rediscovering the first religion I ever believed in. The dream I always had. The moving image of the flesh. Natural transgression. Bodies filled with sexual intensity. All that coming and going between the immense viewing area with its orchestra and balcony and bathrooms. One film. Two films.

The movie stars. Adil Imam. Yousra. Nour Cherif. Leïla Eloui. The Arabic language as a space of origins, a real, mental space where I dared to redefine who I was, dared to talk about everything, reveal everything and one day, write about everything, everything. Even forbidden love. And call it by a new name. A name that had dignity. As if it were a poem.

IV

WRITING

My personal journal from 2002.

A large journal with 96 pages and a very blue cover.

I had lost it.

Yesterday when I was cleaning, I found it again, forgotten, abandoned for who knows how long behind my closet.

In the middle of the journal there was—there is—an envelope with the following title written on it: "The Algerian and the Moroccan."

I knew what was inside. Words, words written by the two of us, the Algerian and me. The story of our love recorded day by day, each alongside the other. Were the words we wrote still intact, legible, or had they been erased over time?

I opened the letter. Once again I opened my heart to the Algerian. I opened my body to his insane story, a great love story, a story built around the greatest and strongest love I have ever known.

There weren't only words in the envelope. Alongside yellowed pages that had been yanked out of another diary, I found four other things. A scrap of paper with the Algerian's phone number on it. A piece of Délice black currant candy. A hotel bill. Two movie tickets for Claire Denis' film *Beau Travail*. Souvenirs? No, more like pieces of evidence. Proof that I really did meet that man. I was 27. He was 36. Nobody in Paris knew I existed back then. But he did. He was God. Right from the start. He was dancing. I joined him. I danced. He loved me. I loved him. For a year and a half, he was my world, my self, my destiny. He was it. Him. Slimane. The guy from southern Algeria, the one with the light skin. The married man who had just left his wife. The father of four girls. Foundry worker. Sculptor. A man with the soul of a poet. An Arab. More of an Arab than me. And crazy, both talkative and uncommunicative at the same time.

Back then, I was living on Oberkampf Street with another man, a French guy named Samy. I had met him in the Paris subway a few days after my arrival in the capital. Whatever love I felt for him had gone sour quickly. We were headed towards a break-up. We just didn't enjoy being together. We fought all the time, used yelling as a weapon, silence as a weapon. I left him the instant I met Slimane. While we were looking for an apartment, the Algerian and I lived in a hotel. The Hotel Aviator, 20 Louis-Blanc Street. Slimane had a house in Strasbourg where his wife and daughters lived. In Paris, he stayed with his brothers. We had nowhere else to go. For two months, the hotel in Paris' 10th arrondissement was our nest, our cage, our home, sweet home. Four walls. Eating, making love. And nothing else. That was our life, that and apartment hunting.

We wound up finding one on Clignancourt Street in the 18th arrondissement. The Marcadet-Poissonniers subway stop on Line 4. It was on the 6th floor and measured 193.75 square feet.

That's where we each became the other's prisoner and fell in love, the place where we spoke Arabic every day, the place where we lived just one step away from madness.

From the start, we wrote sitting next to one another, wrote for one another, one of us telling the story of the other man's life, about his past, his personas, his images, his obsessions. We were able to do an incredible thing, something which would have been impossible with any other person. Two different men writing as it were from a single pen, moving the writing forward by both writing things down, by both being in love and in the writing of love at the same time.

When it ended, in the summer of 2001, Slimane took the two big journals with him before he left, the journals where we had recorded everything, page after page of love. He decided that since I was the one who had broken up with him, he had a right to this "treasure," it belonged to him, the great, misunderstood lover.

Three months later, I found a letter under my door. The same one I'm holding in my hands now. These pages were inside it. A few of the pages I wrote alone in the diary.

Here, all mixed up, and without dates in it, is what Slimane wanted me to remember about him, about us.

On Slimane's forehead there are four wrinkles. On the end of his nose, there's a kind of little "crack." Slimane says his grandmother, Maryam, has one too.

He has a rounded face. And when he talks, almost all his muscles move at the same time and they move a lot. I get caught up in the fascinating mechanics of it all every time I look at him. How his whole face talks.

I go to him, even if he doesn't invite me. I always answer his calls. I move in closer to his face and press my muscles against his.

Slimane's eyes are dark, always dark. Even when they look at me. They entice me. They make me feel shy. They frighten me. I put my head down. I don't want to confront them and I don't want to seduce them—I've already done all that! I want to flow right into them, love them, see myself through their light.

I didn't see him yesterday. He didn't call me. I didn't call him. I didn't dare disturb him. He said he had things to do with his brothers in Aulnay-sous-Bois.

I miss him. I miss everything about him. I close my eyes. I picture him entering the apartment. That's the image I focus on: How he looks when he comes in, how he shows up... His face is still inside the mask he wears in the outside world. He looks up. He smiles, just a little. He looks like himself now. The man he really is, naked, right here, and all mine. I throw the door wide open. I step back a little. This is the one moment I never want to miss. He steps inside and closes the door because he's always the one who closes the door behind us. Closes it behind our two bodies. I'm always the one who makes the first move, who is all over him. Little me. And big him. Me the little guy and him the big guy, big as Chouaïb who almost raped me back when my childhood was ending.

I miss Slimane. It's cold out. I hope he hasn't come down with the flu.

Slimane's mother is named Saïda. He tells me it's a first name that suits her well: she who is happy. But she hasn't always been like that. Her mother-in-law in southern Algeria, taking advantage of her son's early departure to work in France, made her life difficult. Sometimes she would beat her. Slimane grew up being a pawn between the two women. He loves his mother, of course he does. But he absolutely venerates his grandmother. And that situation still causes him problems today. He can't talk to Saïda about his grandmother. About all the stuff they went through together. He talks to me about his grandmother. About Aïcha.

He tells me, "My loving and intimidating Aïcha knew how to talk to stones. She could make them move." He believed her. I can see it in his eyes, he did believe her. I can also see that he misses all the minor miracles he got to witness when he was around that authoritarian woman. Deep down inside, Slimane is still back home. A son of the south, the sand, the wide open spaces. He'll never own up to it but his father committed a crime when he forced him to come to Paris and take over the grocery store in Gennevilliers. He was barely 17 when he went from being the proud man bronzed by the sun to the corner Arab running a store in a bleak neighborhood. It happened about twenty years ago. But in Slimane's mournful eyes, the big move happened only yesterday. Beyond his control. He couldn't say no to his father. To paternal authority. So he brought Aïcha and all her stones along with him.

I am jealous. For two days now, this one name has become part of our daily banter: Saâd. Slimane's best friend back in Algeria. A friend from his childhood years, his adolescence.

Through elementary school, middle school, high school.

For two days, Slimane hasn't talked about anyone else but him. Saâd... Saâd... Saâd... He doesn't say it, but in my mind, I'm convinced they were lovers. All through their boarding school years in middle school and high school, they slept together in the same bed.

Slimane, who is jealousy personified, pays me no mind as he goes on and on about his very dear friend. He can't even imagine that I might get jealous. And that bothers me.

Today in the bookstore on Clichy Square, I found a novel with the same title as the first name of Slimane's close, close friend. Saâd by Alain Blottière. I bought it, but I'm not sharing it with Slimane. Every man has his own Saâd.

Slimane was born on August 11, 1964, in Biskra. He's a Leo. Like me.

I'm waiting for Slimane.

I am Slimane. So taken over by him. Breathing exactly the same way he does. I'm looking through Le Petit Robert *dictionary to try to understand more about him. To relate to him even more. Relate to what he does when he goes to work. To be where I can be with him.*

FOUNDRY:

1. The technique and industry of manufacturing objects by smelting metal and pouring it into molds. A smeltery.

2. A factory where ore is melted down to extract metal. Steelworks. A forge.

3. A workshop where molten metal is used to manufacture certain objects.

FOUNDER:

1. The owner or operator of a foundry.

2. A worker who manufactures objects by smelting.

3. A blast furnace worker who supervises the flow from the smelter.

I try to think back. How things started. What caught my eye.

Back to that night. That nightclub, the one I went to for the first time in my life. The trendy crowd that I didn't really care for.

All of a sudden, Arab music. Warda. The legendary Warda remixed.

The whole atmosphere lightened up. I did too.

He was dancing. Alone. Dancing like they do where he's from. Free and wild. Traditional. Blue. Eyes cast down. Stepping out of another time zone.

I recognized the steps, knew where he was from, exactly where he was from. Algeria.

I moved in closer so I could see him better. Touch him without lifting a hand. Inhale him. Gaze in admiration. And without a move, dance right there with him.

Later on, I became brave and went up and talked to him, complimented him. He looked up and smiled, and I fell for him, instantly, immediately. Like what some people call love at first sight. What I call mutual recognition, how two people recognize they were meant for one another. It's the mektoub *of lovers.*

He didn't say anything. He kept smiling. Smiling at me.

I didn't leave his side. He didn't leave mine. We danced together. One time. A slow dance. Isabelle Adjani's "Navy Blue Sweater."

As the night wore on, we walked around the city together. When we got to Republic Square, I gave him my phone number. He didn't want to give me his.

That didn't bother me. I knew he'd be part of my life forever.

I could wait, I could wait for him. Be patient while my head filled up with images of his sweetness, his virility, the way he spoke Arabic with that southern Algerian accent, the way he smoked, the way his body danced.

I waited three months. Consumed with desire. Totally aroused. Totally in love.

A few days before New Year's Eve 2000, he called.

I dropped everything and moved in with him. Went searching for a place where we could live together. Away from everybody else. From everybody who knew us.

Today is Tuesday.

I've spent the last four days with Slimane. We haven't left the apartment. I've spent four days crawling all over him, four days with him all over me. Eating. Making love. Fighting. Making up. Sleeping. Each inside the other, literally. Prisoners.

It's almost four o'clock. I'm at the movies. I'm going to see Vittorio De Sica's The Bicycle Thief *for the first time. I'm impatient to discover the images. I'm also a little sad. Slimane didn't want to come with me. He preferred to spend time with his brothers, his horrible brothers... I hate them.*

Right before I left, he said, What do you like more, love or movies?

He didn't even give me time to answer.

He must have known what my answer would be, known it better than me.

Slimane only returned a few pages from our journal. He kept the rest for himself, maybe even destroyed them. Burned them. Every last thing we wrote together, one body pressed against the other, our two hands almost joined, writing as if we were a single hand. He took it all, stole all of it for himself. This memoir, this written account of all the time we spent together was now his, his forever. Our book was no longer my book. That really pissed me off. I couldn't help seeing what Slimane did as an attempt at censorship. A way to remove the pages he didn't like. Give me back only the pages he wanted to return, there weren't too many of them, just a few small pages of writing that were, in addition, favorable to him. A way to exclude me. No written trace of me by him. Not a single word he ever wrote about me when we were in love.

I was dispossessed. By cutting sections out, Slimane rewrote our love journal. Misrepresented love. Revealed love in a different light. An incomplete light.

I answered his letter very quickly.

I spent one entire night writing back to him. I came up with a really strange letter where I tried to be logical, terse, cruel, cold, all in vain. I wanted to write a revenge letter, but that's not how it turned out. I mailed it the next day at 7 in the morning. It was early spring. Paris was still dark.

Slimane,

I can't even call you "Dear Slimane" anymore, that's how angry I am. Angry with you. Angry with myself. Angry over the injustice you've imposed. Angry over this thing called love, a concept that doesn't make any sense to me now and yet, love is the thing I'm feeling right now, down in my heart. I'm angry over how you took it upon yourself to play censor to our love journal. Angry because I felt like I gave you my all, every inch of my body and still you were never satisfied.

You wanted more. Always more. Wanted to know everything about me, right down to what I was thinking and what I did when you weren't around. Everything about my heart, the heart I gave you the moment we met. My body had become your body. But you wanted more, more and more and still even more. Well, more of what exactly? I no longer knew what I had left to give… You insisted that I be there for you, always available. And I did that. Was glad to do it. Did it lovingly. Did it with devotion because I loved you. Adored you. I stopped seeing other people, gave up my old life, my imprint on Paris, all my plans, gave up everything and all because of you. I stopped seeing people I really cared about. I mean, who needs friends once you've found love? What could you possibly get from anybody else that you weren't already getting from me? And exactly who are these other people, these people you feel so close to, these people I don't even know? Thousands of questions. I answered all of them, had an explanation for everything. Thousands of questions repeated thousands of times. Some days, I didn't dare answer you. Those were the days when you didn't seem like yourself...

You didn't believe me. In your eyes, I was nothing but a liar, a dishonest person who slept with anything that moved. That's what you used to tell me, that I was a devil, a demon, an evil spirit that you found yourself in love with. Madly in love. "Possessively" in love with. Unhealthily in love with.

Was I the one you left your wife and children for? I never asked you for that. You were already living here in Paris without them when I met you.

Some days you headed off to work at 7 in the morning, your usual time, and then an hour later you'd be back again. "It's scary, but you're the only thing I can think about. You are me. I can't do another thing... except be here with you, here in this apartment, in this bed, here inside this dark space we've created in broad daylight." That happened several times and every time it happened, I'd get choked up, filled with emotion and race to open up the bed, throw some sheets on it, get the pillows and blankets in place, and zip, zip, zip, we'd have our clothes off and there we'd be, pressed up against one another, inhaling one another, and all we'd do was wake up and then fall back asleep again. We practically forgot to eat... Do you remember all that? Of course you do... How could you forget those moments of true love, pure love, times when love was more important and stronger than anything else on earth, anything!

Do you remember the light in my eyes every time I met you at the door? You did notice it one time, just one time. After that, you were caught up in your own concept of what love was about, that what you felt for me was greater than anything I felt for you. The way you acted when you showed up at the apartment every day sent me into shock, a complete upheaval. You'd arrive with barely a smile, sometimes you'd sound playfully ironic and sometimes you'd sound completely grim, and you'd ask me, "Labass, everything cool, Sidi Abdellah?" And I'd look at you and watch the changes that were happening in the air, in the world that had become nothing but You!

I was happy and I was afraid. You were the man in charge, the king. I accepted your authority. I accepted your silences, your reprimands, your theatrics, your obsessions. You'd smoke. I'd sit on the floor and take off your shoes and socks. You never forced me to do that, never. I wanted to do it. Just like I loved to wash your feet in very hot water when it was cold outside, warm them up in that little red basin we'd bought together next to the Stras-bourg-Saint-Denis subway stop. I'd wash them, then dry them off and kiss them: They belonged to me.

You were Algerian, an Arab like me, and you belonged to me. But I could see that you had your doubts, lots of doubts, all the time.

When we first met, you said, "Tell me about the men in your past... what your love life was like before me..." I told you about the boys and men who had been part of my life, told you everything, right down to the smallest detail. You wanted to know everything. Later, much later, you brought up details from that period and ordered, "Renounce your past! Yes, you heard me. Forget about every other guy you were ever with and tell me they weren't worth your time and effort... Tell me the experience you're having with me really is what love is all about and all those other experiences, the ones you had with them, they were only flings, stuff you did for pleasure and fun... Let me hear you say it: Before I met you, I was nothing but a whore! I was looking for love in all the wrong places. Before I met you, I was nothing but a slut! Say it: The past is dead. It does not exist anymore!" It wasn't just a fit of jealousy. You were serious. Your eyes glowed red with hatred, hatred because I had a past, hatred because I had an existence without you. You couldn't stand the thought that I had a life and was happy before I met you. I knew deep down that it wasn't worth trying to convince you otherwise or trying to change the subject. So I said, "Before I met you, I was nothing." And you said, "And tell me that before you met me, you were nothing but a whore!" I said that too. We made love. Both of us crying our eyes out.

Well, it's over now. Over. And this time, I'm the one who broke up with you. The whole business of both of us living by your concept of what love is, both of us being subjected to your possessiveness and your neuroses, all those hang-ups I found so charming and interesting in the beginning, they're over. It is over, even if we still do love one another. I want it to end. I'll say it again and I'll even put it in writing. It is over. I am more than tired of being your love object. Your object, period.

You turned me into the person you wanted me to be. For you, I became a submissive Arab woman. Every day I had to stop whatever I was doing before you came home, sometime around 5, and have everything ready for your comfort and convenience. The tagine made, the mint tea ready. The laundry done... And I swear to you, I swear that I like doing all those things. Washing your dirty clothes, having dinner ready, taking care of your bodily needs. You never forced me to do any of it. And, yes, you contributed to the relationship in any way you could.

The outside world did not exist. For a long time, I tried to see things your way. All I really needed were the feelings that linked us together. The spiritual bond between us was something special, something precious in my eyes. You believed in the same things I did. The saints. The jinns. *Witchcraft. Superstition. Incense. If I talked about the* jaoui, *the* chabba, *the* harmal, *the* fasoukh, *you knew exactly what I meant. Just like you knew that orange blossom water was something I needed in order to survive. Sometimes, I'd get sick. You'd take some of that water and wash my face and hands with it while you chanted a few prayers. It brought me relief. You understood the special state I was in, that hal, the mindset that came over me, and you had the right moves and the right words to bring me out of it, restore me to life, this life in which I loved you. Pressed up against you in bed.*

You did all that for me. And I allowed you to enter my body, enter my soul. What other proof of my love was necessary?

I realize that the average Arab man is complicated. You were a thousand times more complicated than that. I understood you and I did not understand you. I know that love is something bigger than we are. I know that love involves jealousy. Sickness. I've read about it in books. We witnessed it ourselves when we both read The Anthology of Arabic Poetry, *the book you gave me at the beginning of our relationship. We both experienced the same feelings in the course of our two years together. You wanted to be the one in charge. I let you have the power, by my own free will, without thinking about my own future. We were the future, you and I, the two of us linked together, stomach to stomach and heart to heart, by a single breath. I renounced all ambition. I renounced films, the one great dream I had since I was a teenager. Because of you, I stopped pretending that I was tough. I took off the masks, all of them, whenever I was around you. The social identity that I started to build back in Hay Salam ceased to exist once you entered my life. Do you realize that? Are you aware of all my sacrifices? Can't you see that you turned me into a prisoner, a woman imprisoned on Clignancourt Street? No, I don't think you do… You went on having your doubts, subjecting me to your interrogations on a daily basis. I couldn't sit next to you anymore when I played my phone messages. And if, unfortunately, I did do that, I'd have to spend hours and hours explaining everything, who was it that called, how was it that I knew them, had I ever slept with them, why did I keep in touch with them, what did they look*

like physically, what kind of people they were... Everything,
every last thing. I had to tell you everything, be really careful
not to leave out a single detail... It was too much... Intolera-
ble... Impossible...

I have to admit, however, that even when you put me
through hell, part of me was happy, part of me liked what you
were doing, liked the machismo, the dictatorship. I'd keep
telling myself, "This is what love is, this is what love is about...
I am so lucky... All I have to do is hang in there... It's all part
of love..."

I stuck it out as best as I could. I stopped working. I became
your little woman. Your idea of a woman. I became Saâd, your
childhood buddy. I became a lump of clay in your hands. A
body that lived for you, found no other reason to live but you.
An Arab first name, there just for you. A foreign name they
murdered in Paris, but a name you honored. I rediscovered my
own name. And for two entire years, the only thing that mat-
tered was the way you said it. You had the power to bring the
name to life, return it to its Arab nature as no one had done
before. At night, in the dark, we'd fall asleep calling one another
by our first name. Slimane. Abdellah. Slimane. Abdellah. Sli-
mane... I always won the contest. You often fell asleep before I
did. You'd snore a little, let go of my hand, but I'd continue, go
right on praying... Slimane, Slimane, Slimane, Slimane...
And you were this body breathing inside me. I didn't see you. I
recognized you. I inhaled you. I spoke to you in Arabic. In our
language, the language we made love in, a love beyond what
the law allowed.

With you, I became an Arab again and at the same time, went far beyond that identity.

Beyond that race, that culture, that religion. And sex, in that context, made us feel like we were committing a transgression every time we were intimate, made us feel like we were being joined together in heaven, made us feel like we did the first time we made love. Sex with you stopped being just sex. Every inch of you found the place where it belonged on me and inside me. You'd turn shy and start using the dirty words that all bad little boys in Algeria used. I'd feel shy, look down and immediately look up and ask to hear more. They were not insults. My ears heard them as poems, my heart thought of them as a love potion and then, down there, down at the lower end of my stomach, there you were, your body beefy and naked. You were a zamel. *A homo. And I was too. I was your fag and you were mine and we were gay for one another, gay without pride and gay without shame.*

You used to like going to the mosque once in a while. You said you liked the gymnastics that praying involved, liked being in the middle of a crowd of strangers praying, liked how your words gave you a simple and direct connection to God. You stopped going after you met me. You didn't dare go. Islam declared that a bond like the one between us was a sacrilege. You couldn't stop feeling that way. I didn't try to change the way you saw things. I was living with the same contradiction myself. I needed to believe. I wanted to.

We found our own solution. We headed to St. Bernard's and watched other people praying. We had no connection to the churches in the world from where we came, they simply weren't part of our spiritual memory. Yet we visited churches on several occasions and discovered a whole new spirituality. We invented it together, a religion, a faith, a chapel, a dark and luminous corner, a moment in time beyond the boundaries of time. Discovered a Christianity not far from Barbès Boulevard.

I'm getting off track. What I wanted to do was blame you, blame you vastly and here I am, talking about all the good times we had... I'm off track... I must still be in love with you, but I shouldn't. I shouldn't. No way, not anymore. I suffered. I'm still suffering. You're not around anymore, but you're still a big part of me. I can feel it. I let my heart do without you and now I have to learn to live by myself again in solitude. You're here in Paris, not far from me, over in the next neighborhood, the last stop on the RER B Line. I watch you, I follow you. You come in. You go out. I grow detached. I grow attached. I shut my eyes to make you go away, shut them so I can start cursing you out, any day now, but I don't dare... I don't dare...

I don't know how many times you've broken up with me. We'd be fighting. I'm not somebody who gives up easily. I'm a lot like my mother, I can be stubborn, a real dictator when I want to be. You were sick. You were driven by jealousy. You always had to have the last word. I wasn't about to let you have it, at least not that easily. So you'd grab your tools and tell me, "I don't love you anymore. I'm leaving. Go on, go live your life with all those other people, the ones you love more than me..." There was nobody else, nobody else but you. How many times did I have to swear that was the truth, shout it out loud? My whole existence had come down to that. Me shouting, me crying, me making excuses. You would abandon me. Leave. And ten minutes later, I'd come running after you, racing down all the streets in the 18th arrondissement. Down Clignancourt Street. Barbès Boulevard. Doudeauville Street. Down to the little bridge. Down to the little bench. That's where you'd be waiting. Sitting there on the little bench. I'd catch up with you. We'd sit together, watch the trains go by from the Gare du Nord station. Sit in silence. The black African immigrants, the ones we loved, the ones who touched us for reasons we couldn't figure out, they'd walk past us, do the talking for both of us. Yell for me when I couldn't. Intercede with you on my behalf and not even realize it. Once again, you'd start to smile. You'd come back to your senses. And then, very calmly, we'd get up and, same as always, head off to buy some melon, your favorite fruit. Then we'd come back to Clignancourt Street and celebrate our appeased love. Miles away from madness, at least for the moment.

But the same madness always showed up again and consequently, it destroyed something inside me. You were crazy. I was too, but a lot less crazy than you.

In the end, you simply wore me out. Exhausted me. After a year and a half of an intense affair, a possessed love, I didn't have the strength to repeat the same old stories, to withstand your authority, to be less in love than you.

Over time, you managed to put the thought in my head that my love was somehow inferior to yours. You were a mystical poem. I was nothing but a Guy de Maupassant novella... It's true, you were a love machine, I could see that, see it right from day one. I was always lagging behind, constantly racing just to keep up with you, somehow match your level of intensity, even a little. You have no idea the price I paid for doing that. You never even noticed how hard I was trying. Never rewarded my efforts. When it comes down to it, you never once thought about the solitude you were forcing me into, all that isolation in the name of love... And really, when it comes down to it, you were right. There always was a small part of me that opposed your will and I'm sure you were well aware of the fact before I was, and it was the small defiance that made you suffer, quite literally made you sick and crazy.

I could not let my dreams of Paris vanish completely. I was in the city to grow up, become an adult. Be somebody. Make a name for myself. To finally turn my dreams into reality, all the ideas I had about life, about making movies, the dreams I'd been carrying around inside me for so long, for too long. You never understood that. I didn't either, never knew how strong the dreams were. That they were THE strongest thing of all. To find love, a love you can proclaim in Arabic, that's an unexpected miracle. But I couldn't talk to you about all the things I wanted to do with my life. About all the things that were bigger than I was. So I kept quiet. I hid that stuff without realizing it, without planning on it. I didn't speak to you. I spoke to Paris.

I confess, admit it openly. Your love was the purest one. But it was the kind of love that requires the other person to be in top physical shape, another form of madness I don't possess. I gave it my all. I gave everything. Compared to the wealth of things you have to offer, I am nothing but a poor man. A nobody compared to you, a man so sure of himself, so in touch with his vision. I am small, small-time, a little guy. One minute you'd put me up on a pedestal and then you'd push off. You dumped me one time too many. After hitting the ground so many times, my legs couldn't break another fall.

I went looking elsewhere. You pushed me to that point.

I had to end it. Cheat on you.

It happened, down in the lower level of the Gare de l'Est train station. He was a baker. Different from you in every way. Blond. Thin. Very young. From Lille. The whole thing lasted maybe fifteen minutes. Fifteen minutes to get covered with dirt, go back to the way I lived before I met you, let myself go at it, go at it all by myself. A brief moment of meaningless sex, an opportunity to commit a sin and walk away from our religion, turn my back on Christ and His churches.

I did it. I knew what I was doing. I did things with that guy that I never did with you. New moves. New things. Risky stuff. A lot of violence. Darkness, but not the kind we shared.

I went home. I waited for you. I didn't make dinner. You cooked something when you came back from work. We ate. For the first time, I picked a fight with you. I knew what to say, had planned it all out, knew exactly how to make you feel crazy, to make you feel like getting the hell out of there, like breaking up with me, breaking up right then and there.

You left.

I didn't stop you.

You walked the streets, crossed the boulevard. Alone. The night was still young. It was about bedtime.

How many hours did you sit on that little bench of ours down near the bridge while you waited for me? Did you cry? How long did it take you to figure out that it was over, that I wasn't coming back? Were the Africans hanging out with their music and their dancing?

How many packs of cigarettes did you smoke? When you ran out of them, what did you do? Sit, sit waiting, sit watching the trains go by?

I know you didn't cry. You never cry. You just shut down. I'm the one who has to come to you, open you back up to the world again, open you back up to yourself. That night, I didn't come to get you. Come to take you back, just the way you are. Come to love you in spite of everything, love you in spite of my own feelings.

In the strange darkness of our apartment, I was awake all night. I was in a state of total shock. You'd never be here again, here in this light, here beside me. I drove you away. It was me who took back all the power I once allowed you to wield over me. I didn't know what to do with it.

Like you, I didn't cry.

Like you, I went back to being a man from a faraway place. Back to being an Arab image of a man. Distant. Proud. Harsh. A little puppet. Someone who was plain ridiculous.

Like you, I smoked. I smoked for the first time in my life. They were your cigarettes. A pack you forgot, a pack I valued and very carefully hid.

Your cigarettes were strong. They burned my throat. I couldn't breathe anymore. But I smoked every last one of them, didn't even open the window to air the place out. I wanted to suffocate. Smother the both of us. Wanted a haze to come rolling in, settle like fog between us. Act like a wall. A prison. A new prison, a prison built just for me.

I was inside all that darkness, inside that execution, that willed death, and I thought about my sister, the one who was possessed. I summoned her jinns. *And they came. I stood up. They entered me. I fell down.*

Elsewhere, I had a dream.

I was in Cairo, the only city we ever planned to visit together one day, and I was finally crying, telling our story to the city's many ruins.

I had already forgiven you.

I had already known that I'd never get over you.

That I was going to turn nostalgic.

Always immersed in the way you loved.

You cut stuff out of our journal. You took out what bothered you. And me? You left me a few scraps. It's like you changed the things that really happened, made everything turn out your way. With lots of hate. With your cold stare. You rewrote history. You had to be the alpha male, the guy who, once again, went on being right. You have all the rights, isn't that how it works... even the right to have the last word every single time? I want you to know, right here, right now, that starting tonight and for that matter, from here on out, I am convinced that none of this really matters. It's not important. I'm not being proud. It's all very clear now, clear as day, despite the darkness and the suffering.

Someday I'm going to rehash all of this, maybe in a film, maybe in another dream. I'll tell the whole thing my way, from my point of view. All the pages you cut out, the ones you kept for yourself, they'll all come back to me. All I'll have to do is follow the few tracks that remain, the prints in the desert that used to be our love.

I'm no longer myself.

I am possessed by you and will be possessed forever. You know that... you do. There's a part of me that will always belong to you forever. You know that... figured it out before I did. I'm going to have to live with that fact. It's you and me, we're both in there. No matter how I feel about it. Whether I am conscious. Absent. Day after day. Year after year.

Kisses.

Kisses to you and... and, that's it.

Abdellah

Exactly one year after I wrote the letter to Slimane, I received an answer from him. An orphan of a poem. Just a poem. Not a single word with it. It was an Arabic poem, of course, one from another era, a poem written by a mythical poet of the 8th century, a man remembered for his blindness, his considerable ugliness, his atheism, his poetic genius. He has a beautiful name: Bashār ibn Burd. And his poem, "Cruel Games," is a classic in Arabic poetry.

> *I do lament*
> *those who granted me*
> *one taste of their affection,*
> *and once my desire was aroused,*
> *nodded off to sleep.*

> *They urged me to stand*
> *up,*

and once I did,
bravely bearing the burden
that their affection
imposed,
they hastened thereafter to
sit.

Thus I shall exit this world,
and leave behind your love
still thriving within my chest,
beneath my emaciated ribs
where no one will ever
notice its presence.

Unto sadness
I am bound,
closely, closely, and never
will our long relationship end,
unless some day an eternity itself,
doth cease to be.

ABOUT THE AUTHOR

Abdellah Taïa (b. 1973) is the first openly gay autobiographical writer published in Morocco. Though Moroccan, he lives in Paris. His novels have been translated into Spanish, Italian, German, and Dutch. He also appeared in Rémi Lange's 2004 film *Tarik el Hob* (released in English as *The Road to Love*).